THE FRIEND WHO LIED

A GRIPPING PSYCHOLOGICAL THRILLER

RACHEL AMPHLETT

SAXON
PUBLISHING

1

LISA

I'M ALIVE.

It's the first thought that enters my head as I open my eyes, my eyelids sticky with dried tears.

I can't focus.

It's dark; I can sense that much. There's a silence around me that suggests it's night-time – a stillness that cloaks the space.

I can breathe easily. My mouth and nose aren't covered with anything, but then an overwhelming light-headedness seizes me and I scrunch up my eyes to ward it off.

The muscles down my right side are tight and painful, as if I've been punched in the stomach. There's bile at the back of my throat, a bitter taste that nauseates me, and I wrinkle my nose in disgust.

I don't want to be sick.

I try to speak but all I can do is mumble as if I've forgotten how to form complete sentences. Even simple words are beyond me.

Where am I?

Why am I here?

I lick my lips. They're dry and cracked. My throat aches as if I haven't swallowed for an age.

A clatter of metal on metal shatters the silence, and my heart lurches as I fight against the panic that seizes me.

I strain my ears to listen to what follows. I'm scared to breathe in case I miss it, so I count to ten, then twenty.

That's when I hear the echo.

It's faint at first as my brain tries to latch on to what I'm listening to. A distant *beep* and pressure on my arm.

The fog lifts a moment, and I remember blue flashing lights, grim faces, a police officer taking notes and talking in a low tone.

The thought escapes as quickly as it appears, and my head lolls to one side, my eyelids heavy once more.

TWO HOURS, four?

I don't know.

I wipe at swollen eyes, scared at my weakness, my inability to stay awake.

I sense others around me, beyond the periphery of my limited vision, and my heart rate ratchets up a notch.

Why are they here?

The light changes as a blurred figure moves past my feet with an efficiency borne of necessity, and I begin to understand.

And then I'm clawing my way out of the darkness, my eyes opening, squinting in the dim light that fills the room.

As the blurry outline approaches the bed and bends over me, before I see her lips move and the words form, I realise the awful truth.

If I'm alive, then someone else has died.

2

LISA

THE NURSE SMILES as she finishes taking my temperature and I fight down my embarrassment, colour flaming my cheeks.

Minutes ago, she removed the catheter that had been inserted during the operation, so we're well acquainted now, thank you very much.

'Do you think you could manage some juice?' she says, oblivious to my discomfort.

I nod. 'Please.'

My throat constricts with anticipation. I've been sipping water all morning, and I'm bored. I need something sweet. Something that will trickle over my tongue and ease away the furriness that remains from being unconscious for so long.

Only the pain in my abdomen keeps me from

throwing back the bedcovers and escaping to help myself to the juice.

Rain lashes against the window at the far end of the ward, and if I crane my neck, I can see the tops of the naked horse chestnut trees that surround the hospital car park, their branches stark against a churning grey sky.

On cue, the glass shudders as a blast of November wind punches against it and howls with contempt when it can't reach inside.

I pull the blanket up closer to my chin, pausing my escape plan for the time being, and seeking warmth from the sheets instead.

The nurse checks her watch, scrawls a note across the clipboard in her hand and tweaks something on the machine near my shoulder, then turns to the next in line as she pulls one of the curtains closed, shutting out half of my meagre view.

I sigh and lean my head back on the pillow, listening to the soles of her shoes squeaking as she works her way across the ward to the next patient, then wince as the movement pulls my beat-up muscles.

Part of me is tempted to lift the gown and take a look, but the other half of me is too terrified to contemplate what might be down there. Once I know, there's no going back.

I can guess what's happened, but denial is a fine place to be.

The surgeon didn't talk much when he came around earlier. He lifted my gown, poked and prodded, spoke to his junior staff who trailed around after him like a motley collection of ducklings, and then shot off out of the ward and down the corridor, the ducklings in his wake.

I don't need to imagine what the bruises look like. I can feel each and every one of them.

Apparently, some people hardly bruise at all. Some people can be out of bed within twenty-four hours.

Some people are freaks.

I can hear the nurse at the far end of the ward now, making her way past each and every one of us, taking the time to check we're all right. I can't see her now the curtain has been pulled. I can only see beyond my feet and to the right towards the window. I can't see what's going on in the ward, or out in the corridor.

My blinkered view creates a cocoon that suffocates and compresses my thoughts.

It'll be at least another twenty minutes before I see that juice.

I stare at the damp patch on the ceiling and try to work out if it's widened since I last looked at it half an hour ago. It might be an old stain, but I want to be sure. Its uneven edges trace across the plasterwork like an ancient map seeking new adventures, and I'm reminded of books I read as a kid: fantastical stories that described battles and quests across mystical lands.

There's a commotion over near the door, and I prop myself up on my elbows, my breath catching in my throat.

I hear murmurs as they approach.

'It's unprecedented.'

My dad sounds confused; my mum efficient. As always.

They're moving closer.

'Unusual, but—'

'It'll break her heart.'

It's as if they've forgotten that I'm nearly twenty-seven, that I'm an adult, that I'm here, that I'm capable – *am I?* – of making my own decisions.

'She'll find out anyway. One of them will tell her.'

My patience snaps.

'Tell me what?'

The curtain is brushed aside before the surgeon peers in.

I'm surprised to see him again.

His smile is faint; he probably thought I was asleep, resting after the trauma my broken body has been through. 'Your parents are here.'

Having stated the obvious, he steps to one side.

My mum's face breaks my heart, and the way my dad's hand shakes as he reaches out for me leaves me speechless for a moment.

They've been crying, but force smiles. Relief, happiness and hope have replaced the worry lines they've worn these past twelve months. Despite being only in their early sixties, they appear older than their years.

It's now that I realise my illness has affected those around me much more than I've anticipated. I've been so wrapped up in my own grief for my shortened lifespan, I've forgotten what it has inflicted on them.

They've already been through so much – at three years old, I'd been diagnosed with a heart condition. And now, this.

Dad's not usually one for grand gestures but he's the first to the side of the bed, wrapping me in a bear hug the likes of which I haven't had since I was a toddler.

When he releases me, Mum is dabbing a tissue to her eyes.

As we embrace, I feel tears damp against my cheek.

'It's okay, Mum. I'm okay.'

Mum wraps her fingers around my hand and squeezes. 'You got a new kidney, love. They say the operation was a success, and you should be able to come home soon.'

'How?'

It's not the stupid question you might think it is.

Three weeks ago, I was told to prepare for the worst. Three weeks ago, none of this was a factor in my life. Three weeks ago, I'd given up.

We had driven here in silence then. The return trip was worse – I had to put my earbuds in so that I couldn't hear my mum's quiet sobs over the dull thrum of the car engine.

Now, the surgeon speaks first.

'Unusual circumstances,' is all he says.

'That's impossible. You said there was no hope.'

My gaze travels from him to my parents, then back.

Mum and Dad look at each other, and I see the fear in their eyes.

The knowledge that it's up to them to tell me because the surgeon isn't saying anything. That they know there's no going back from this moment. It won't be undone; whatever they're about to tell me can't be unsaid.

'Who?' I ask, terrified of the answer as soon as the question passes my lips.

Mum shakes her head and turns away, then Dad strokes my hair and says—

'I'm sorry, love. It was Simon. Simon died.'

3

LISA

Mum and Dad left half an hour ago.

I'm not supposed to know who my donor is. That's not how it's supposed to work, but someone made a mistake and let it slip within earshot of my parents.

Someone is probably looking for a new job right now.

Since they left, I've been staring at that stain in the plasterwork above the bed opposite me, trying not to panic.

No-one's answering my texts or calls, and I don't go on social media. I haven't used it for years.

Mum and Dad didn't give me any details. I was too upset to listen anyway, and now I'm angry with myself. I should've asked, no matter how much it would have hurt to know.

I look up from my clenched hands at the sound of a steady shuffle, and see the old lady from the bed two along from mine walking past in her slippers, clutching an IV stand as if to anchor herself.

I wonder if she should be up and about.

My suspicions are confirmed when one of the nurses bustles forward, all efficiency and bossiness, gently demanding to know what the woman is doing out of bed, and where she's going.

'I want to go home.'

The woman's bottom lip wobbles, and I look away, embarrassed.

I want to go home, too. I want to hide away and pretend that none of this is happening, and that Simon is still alive.

The nurse steers the woman back to her bed, coaxing her to do what she's told in the way only health workers can, her voice cheerful while she tucks in the blankets and rests her hand on the old woman's.

I turn my attention to the bed on my left as soft snores emanate from a layer of sheets and blankets, the only sign of the occupant a shock of greying black hair.

A woman in the bed opposite smiles at me, her features too eager, too open, her hands clasped on top of an open gossip magazine. She'll want to know why I'm here, what happened, everything.

I close my eyes. I don't want to talk to her.

I don't want to talk to anyone right now.

I want to remember Simon.

Raven-haired, green-eyed, and my first teenage crush.

I remember the first day he appeared at the steel gates leading into the paved yard of the grammar school, his bag slung over his shoulder and his tie askew, wearing a glare for anyone he caught staring at him. An air of rebellion radiated from him as he stalked towards the classroom.

Not enough to get reported; just enough to make heads turn.

Our school was a dark brick and low-slung construction, the last building added in the early 1970s when the local council realised just how fast their population was increasing.

Black painted railings separated us from the street beyond, with the gates propped open between two red-brick pillars during term time. One gate bore signs banning anyone entering from smoking or driving over five miles per hour.

The cracked and pitted asphalt of the break area fell silent as he passed, conversations forgotten as we watched him wrench open the door to the scuffed and pockmarked building that housed the science block, and then disappear without a backward glance.

I smile to myself at the memory.

He had a dimple at the side of his mouth. Only on the left, not the right. He didn't smile often; not in that full unbridled joyous way that most people do. When Simon smiled, it had a cool and calculating air about it, as if he knew something you didn't and he'd get a kick out of it when you finally found out.

He somehow breezed through sixth form without drawing the attention of the bullies or the cool kids. He simply hovered at the edges, observant.

It took six months to break through the icy exterior he maintained, and it wasn't me that did it.

It was him.

I loved the art classes at school. I loved the fact that I got to spend three hours of uninterrupted bliss creating something. It was where I found my calling, and I was determined to get a university place based on the strength of my growing portfolio of work.

It was one of the few classes where we all got on reasonably well with the teacher, too. I can't remember his name now but he had the habit of playing seventies rock music in the background while we worked and somehow that seemed to take the wind out of the sails of any of the potential troublemakers.

I was trying to use acrylics to emulate a still-life photograph I'd cut out of my dad's Saturday newspaper supplement, when I became aware of a presence at my elbow.

I glanced up and almost dropped the paintbrush in surprise when I found Simon hovering there, transfixed by the painting.

'That's quite good,' he said, then pointed at the wine bottle to which I'd been adding shadow. 'If you add a hint of white there, it'll sort out the perspective better.'

My natural reaction would have been to argue the point if it was anybody else, but this was Simon. I was too shocked at his speaking to me to do anything else but what he suggested.

And, damn it, he was right.

I took a step back from the easel and, just for a moment, felt a rush of adrenalin that it had worked. I turned to find him grinning at me, that dimple on the left-hand side out of sight.

I smiled back. 'Thanks.'

'No problem.' He gestured to the paintbrush. 'Can I have that now? They're all gone and I need one that size.'

I handed it over, disappointed that he'd only thought to help me because I had what he wanted.

But I'd have done anything for him, I would.

I frown as another memory resurfaces of Simon, who was alive the last time I saw him.

I twist my head, trying to see where the nurse has gone but she's out of sight, and I don't want to push the button next to the bed. I've seen how hard she and her colleagues work on this ward.

I try to tamper down my frustration, but it's there bubbling away under the surface, threatening to turn to panic.

What happened to Simon?

Why did he die?

4

LISA

'LISA!'

I manage a smile as I set eyes on the petite blonde who bounds across the tiled floor towards me.

At once, I wish I'd had the chance to brush my teeth or run a comb through my hair.

Hayley Matthews is dressed immaculately in a cream trouser suit and white blouse, an air of efficiency in her step as she shoves her car keys into her bag and then lowers herself into the chair beside my bed.

'You nearly missed visiting hours,' I say, not unkindly.

She has a habit of turning up late, but despite this we all love her. No matter her own troubles, she's the one amongst the five of us who can always raise a smile.

Four of us, I remind myself.

She places her bag on the floor, twitches a tendril of hair behind her ear and leans closer, lowering her voice.

'Sorry I haven't had a chance to text you back. How are you doing?'

I shrug, then wince as my stomach muscles protest at the movement. 'The doctor says I'm doing well. He reckons I'll be discharged within a few days. They're just trying to get the anti-rejection doses right at the moment, before I can be released.'

Her perfectly groomed eyebrows shoot upwards. 'That soon?'

'It's normal for something like this these days.'

'Wow.'

Her expression softens, her bottom lip trembling, and I hold up my hand.

'Mum and Dad were here earlier. They told me.'

'Oh, Lisa – I'm so sorry.' She pulls a paper tissue from her handbag and dabs at her eyes. 'It can't be easy. I mean, you're not supposed to know who your—'

'I know.'

Hayley sniffs, then shoves the tissue back in her bag and straightens. She leans forwards and wraps her fingers around mine. Her nails are a dainty shade of pink. 'Do they think it worked?'

I exhale and rest my head on the pillow, avoiding the gaze of the nosy old lady in the bed opposite who's been trying to engage me in conversation for the past three hours. I don't want to know about her four cats, or her errant son-in-law. I've already heard her tell everyone else in the ward since the effects of the anaesthetic wore off, and I'm tempted to ask to be knocked out again if she starts talking to me.

'Yes. It's early days, obviously, but they say the operation went well. The kidney seems to be doing what it should, and my numbers look good.'

She brightens for a moment. 'That's great, Lisa. Really great.'

'What happened?' I lower my voice to a whisper because Nosy Woman is doing her best to catch my attention. 'What went wrong in the escape room?'

Hayley glances across at the other patient, then stands and pulls the curtains closed around my bed to give us some privacy.

I smile as she sits back in the chair. 'That'll drive her up the wall.'

'Good.' She nibbles at the skin at the side of her thumbnail before dropping her hand to her lap. 'Have the police spoken to you?'

'What? No – why?'

'Don't worry about it.' She shrugs. 'They're probably waiting until you feel better.'

With the curtain closed, it seems like we're cut off from the rest of the world, and the space between us shrinks.

I'm suddenly overwhelmed by the perfume Hayley's wearing. It's new, and too musky; not the usual scent she wears. She's agitated, too. Fidgeting. She twists the second of three studs in her left earlobe; a habit I haven't seen her doing in years. Not since we left university, that's for sure.

'Hayley? What happened?'

'Can't you remember?'

I shake my head and dig my fingernails into my palms. 'I keep trying, but all I can remember is that there were a lot of flashing lights, and then it went dark. Bits and pieces come back to me, but it's like I can't keep hold of the memory.'

'I expect that's the effect of the anaesthetic. It'll take time.'

She reaches over and tops up my water glass for me, and it's a moment before I realise she still hasn't answered my question.

Her jaw is clenched; I can see the muscles tighten as she sets down the glass and then fusses with her bag, pulling out her mobile phone before giving a slight shake of her head.

I'm staring at her as she raises her gaze to mine, and then opens her mouth.

Too late.

The curtain is pushed aside and the ward sister, Delia, glares at both of us.

'If you close the curtain completely, I can't keep an eye on you. It's for your own safety.'

'Sorry,' I mumble.

Delia tuts, then turns her attention to Hayley. 'Visiting hours finished five minutes ago. You'll have to come back tomorrow.'

Hayley's expression is hard to define.

At first, I think she's embarrassed, but then I realise the truth.

She's relieved.

She doesn't have to tell me what happened.

She pushes herself out of the chair, swipes her bag from the floor and shoves her phone into it before giving me a breezy peck on the cheek.

'You look great, Lisa. I've got to go.'

She brushes past Delia without a backward glance, and I shrug.

'She runs her own business. She's busy.'

Delia shakes her head as she tucks the curtain back against the wall, then turns away. 'Get some rest.'

I watch her stalk across the ward to another of her charges – a middle-aged woman who had her appendix out two days ago – and Nosy Woman. I quickly lose interest; I'm too confused by Hayley's reluctance to talk.

Out of all of us, she's usually the biggest gossip. Her capacity to talk knows no bounds. Despite the terrible, awful fact that Simon has died, she'd normally want to make sure I knew what was going on.

Now?

Now there's a barrier between us, and one of Hayley's making.

Whatever happened to Simon, whatever happened to me, isn't going to come from her.

I'm going to have to try to remember.

5

HAYLEY

A CLOYING STENCH of sweat and old food lingers on the overheated air.

It reminds me of school dinners in a cramped canteen, of damp changing rooms after hockey matches, and I can't breathe.

A nurse bustles past, the crisp uniform she wears crackling as she swings her arms, propelling herself across the tiled floor towards one of the beds.

A middle-aged couple sit huddled in chairs next to a teenage girl in the last bed on the ward, their murmured conversation drowned out by the squeak of a trolley that's wheeled along the corridor by a lanky man with thinning black hair. His pace is unhurried, his eyes vacant as he fights a losing battle against a wonky wheel. The trolley rolls to the left, and he pauses to adjust its course before setting off once more, the squeak fading into the distance.

My heels are too noisy on the tiled floor; my footsteps echo off the beige walls as I breathe through parched lips.

Sweat itches at my temples and the nape of my neck. I tug at the silk scarf that I wore to set off the cream-coloured blouse I chose to wear, then scrunch it up and stuff it into the tan leather tote bag I cradle over one arm.

My hands are shaking before I've escaped the ward.

I pass through thick wooden double doors that have glass partitions three quarters of the way up and my reflection peers back at me for a split second.

I'm taken aback by how calm I look.

The doors swing shut.

My heart rate is pulsing in my ears, accompanied by a rushing sound that makes me blink to try to lose the spots in my vision. I still have to drive home, and I can't do that if I can't see properly. I can't be stranded here, of all places.

The stench of damp cabbage is replaced by

burnt coffee beans; the sign for a coffee franchise pokes out from an open doorway and I peer inside.

There are four or five tables, filled with visitors, hospital workers and who knows who else. Each of them is avoiding eye contact with the other, as if fearful a conversation might be attempted by the other person.

I wrinkle my nose as I reach the counter. I can read the prices from here, and as I watch a splat of dark liquid eject from a machine on the back wall into a cardboard cup, I decide I can wait until I get home.

I turn on my heel and hurry away.

The corridor ends in a T-junction ahead of me and colour-coded signs hang from the ceiling pointing to the Accident and Emergency ward, X-ray department and – thankfully – the exit.

I need fresh air.

The crackle of a radio from around the corner reaches me and I stop dead in my tracks next to a gurney with an elderly man on it.

He peers up at me with quizzical grey eyes, swaddled in pale-yellow blankets, his mouth trembling as he tries to form words.

There is no one with him.

The radio spits to life again – a barked

instruction that peters out as the volume is adjusted, and then a male voice murmurs a short response.

I swallow as my hand dives into my bag and wraps around the spiky cold surface of a bunch of keys.

The car park is only a few metres away, but it seems like miles.

I look around for the police, wondering if they're here.

I don't want to talk to them again. I spoke with them at the escape room, two men in uniform who wore concerned expressions and spoke with an efficiency that frightened me. Then yesterday, a woman – a detective – knocked on my front door and asked all the same questions over again, her eyes suspicious.

She went away, eventually.

But I know she'll be back.

Movement out of the corner of my eye snags my attention. The old man is trying to reach out to me, his eyes beseeching.

I step away from him, and his hand drops to his side as I square my shoulders.

I can't stay here.

I have to get out.

I flick my hair over my shoulder and stalk around the corner, then almost stumble.

It's not the police.

Two paramedics in dark-green jumpsuits are at the nurses' station, chatting with a porter in blue overalls. The older of the paramedics, a woman with fashionably spiky black hair, is leaning against the wall with a clipboard in her hand while her male colleague – who looks about sixteen – holds a walkie-talkie to his mouth, his words clipped and concise.

I pick up my pace. There is nothing to be feared here for now.

I manage a smile at the woman as I pass, then the automatic glass double doors swish open, parting to let me through.

A cold blast of air smacks my nose and cheeks, whisking away my fear for a moment as I concentrate on making my way across a zebra crossing and then the poorly lit asphalt expanse towards my car.

It sits under a pyramid of light cast by a yellowing street light, a shimmer sparkling on the ground from fresh rainfall. Ozone has scorched the air around me, and I gulp it in, remembering summer storms and ruined barbecues, the reality still several months away.

I sink behind the steering wheel, push the key into the ignition and stare at the exit from which I've escaped.

Beyond the glass doors, the two paramedics advance towards the exit, their movements hurried, but determined. There is no indication of panic as they leave the hospital and head towards one of the ambulances parked on the concrete apron outside the doors.

The siren wails once they reach the main road, and I grip the steering wheel as I gasp for air in between sobs that catch in my chest.

It wasn't meant to be like this.

It was never meant to be like this.

6

LISA

THE MINUTE I set eyes on the two police officers that enter the ward the next morning, a shiver crosses my neck and shoulders.

The male police constable wears a uniform with a bulky vest over the top of it. The pockets of the vest bulge with equipment: a radio is clipped to the right hand side, and a set of handcuffs hang from a clip underneath it.

He gives me the briefest of smiles before closing the curtains – he's obviously charmed Delia. He stands next to the wall and reaches into the utility vest that looks like it weighs half a ton, then extracts a small black notebook and pen.

I twist my neck to find the woman on the left-hand side of the bed, her jaw set. She's wearing a charcoal-grey suit that does nothing to offset the harsh brown dye she wears in her hair. She blinks once, then forces a smile.

I'm reminded of a Rottweiler.

'Miss Ashton – Lisa – I'm Detective Constable Angela Forbes. This is my colleague, PC Steve Phillips. How are you feeling?'

'Sore.'

I'm not lying. I know Doctor Ashwan has what he calls my "best interests" at heart, but my abdomen aches like hell and it's swollen from the gas they used to inflate it during the operation.

Normal, he says, for someone who had a new kidney transplanted only three days ago. And for someone he has every intention of kicking out of hospital within days, if everything continues to go as well as it has so far.

I shake my head to clear my thoughts because the Rottweiler is talking, and I've missed half of what she's said.

'Am I under arrest?' I blurt.

The Rottweiler – Forbes, I remind myself – frowns. 'No. This is a formal interview though, so that's why I've had to caution you.'

So, Hayley was right.

They *are* treating Simon's death as suspicious.

But why?

I wince as a bolt of pure fire shoots across my stomach, waves of pain rippling across my body.

'Are you okay?'

The male officer – Phillips – steps forward, concern etched across his features.

I grit my teeth and nod, sweat pooling at my brow. 'Part of the healing process, according to the doc.'

Forbes grimaces. 'Sounds like he should try it himself before making a statement like that.'

I can't help myself, and snort.

Turns out the Rottweiler has a sense of humour after all.

'What did you want to ask me about?'

She pulls the visitor chair across the tiled floor and turns it around to face me before dropping into it with an ill-disguised sigh.

'We're investigating the death of Simon Granger,' she says. 'I realise it's highly unusual for patients to know who their donor was, but as we understand it, he was your final hope, wasn't he?'

I bite my lip, then nod, tears prickling at the corners of my eyes. 'Why are you investigating his death?'

'It's just a routine enquiry,' she says.

'What do you want to know?'

Forbes leans back in her seat. 'Why don't we start at the beginning? Why were you at the A-Maze Escape Room?'

'It was to celebrate my birthday,' I say. I swallow. 'It was meant to be my last one, just in time to join the twenty-seven club alongside Cobain and Winehouse.'

She doesn't register the sarcasm. 'Who organised it?'

'The gang. It was a surprise.'

'Who do you mean by "the gang"?'

'Everyone who was there. Hayley, Bec, Simon and David.'

'Can you explain your health situation at the time?'

'My kidneys were failing,' I say, keeping it simple for her. I'm acutely aware of how much medical jargon I've absorbed osmosis-like these past eleven months. 'If I didn't receive a donor kidney within the next four to six weeks then I'd get more and more sick, until—'

I stop and take a deep breath. There's a rushing sound in my ears as the reality catches up with me.

I should be dead.

Not Simon.

'Do you need a glass of water?' Phillips steps forward.

I shake my head. 'No. Sorry. I just—'

The concern on his face remains. 'Weren't your parents a match?'

'No, and I don't have any siblings.'

'They couldn't offer you dialysis?'

'There were complications – my heart is too weak to cope.'

That's putting it mildly. By the time Doctor Ashwan had finished listing all the reasons why the dialysis option was off the table, both Mum and Dad were crying.

I remember the numbness that had started in my fingers and slowly crawled up my arms and across my body until it was all I could do not to scream.

'Why were you given Simon Granger's kidney?' Phillips says. 'I thought transplant lists meant it was a first-come, first-served basis.'

His question is naïve, but one I would've asked myself if I wasn't so familiar with the process now.

'You're right. We were both brought here from the escape room. My surgeon said he was carrying a donor card,' I say, 'and I was the best match on the donor list.'

'Convenient,' says Forbes. 'If you were so ill, how did you manage go to the A-Maze Escape Room to play with your friends?'

My head whips around.

Forbes is leaning forwards once more, her gaze predatory.

'Pardon?' I'm shocked at the underlying menace of her question.

'If your health was so bad, how were you able to go to the escape room with your friends?'

'Because I was doped up to the nines on painkillers,' I snap. I force myself to relax. 'The doctor agreed to it. By that time, they were already talking about end-of-life choices for me. They didn't know how long I had once the dialysis was off the table. So, the thought of one last birthday with the gang was what kept me going. I thought it'd be my last chance.'

Forbes jerks her chin at my prone body. 'Looks like you got a birthday present as well.'

Her insensitivity shocks, and I force myself up into a sitting position, even though it hurts like hell.

I know I've pushed my luck the moment the monitor next to me starts bleeping wildly.

'I lost a good friend at the weekend,' I snarl.

'I'm not sure what you're insinuating here, but I don't like your tone.'

PC Phillips holds up his hand. 'It's simply routine enquiries.'

'No, it's not. This is harassment.'

I'm saved from another comment from the Rottweiler as the curtain whips open and Delia stands on the threshold, glaring.

'What's going on in here?'

Forbes pushes to her feet and does her best attempt at a sweet smile. 'We were just leaving.'

Delia says nothing, stands to one side to let the two officers pass, and then turns to me, her gaze softening before she hurries across to the bed and helps me lie down once more.

I'm crying by the time we're done, liquid fire seizing my stomach muscles and the wounds that have barely healed.

Delia squeezes my hand. 'You're due some more pain relief in half an hour, not before.'

'Will they be coming back?' I whisper.

She shrugs. 'I suppose it depends how their enquiries go. You could always ask for someone to be present with you next time if you're worried about them.'

I shake my head and force a smile as she retreats.

I don't want to contemplate having to speak to Forbes again, but the reality is that if they've decided to investigate Simon's death then it's likely she'll be back.

But the thought of talking to her with a solicitor present seems ominous.

After all, it's not like I've got anything to hide.

I'M SIPPING room-temperature orange juice the next morning when there's a knock on the door.

David peers around it, his brown eyes lighting up when he sees me.

His is the type of face that is not handsome, but not bad-looking either. He's the sort of person who can fade into the background of a group photograph, unnoticed and unremarkable, despite being six foot tall. There's a stillness about him that none of the rest of us can emulate or understand.

He clutches a cycling helmet in one hand, his black hair sticking up in tufts that mirror the air vents in the helmet, and I glance down at his feet.

He's wearing trainers, not cycling shoes.

'Yeah, I didn't think it'd be a lot of fun walking across these tiles in cleats,' he says.

'Good job you put tracksuit bottoms on, too.'

'There's nothing wrong with Lycra.'

I roll my eyes. 'You're not the one who has to look at it.'

I say the words with a smile, teasing. There's a gentleness about him that I've always put down to shyness, a wariness that only appears around strangers and new places. Out of all my friends, he's the one who is the best listener. A good friend, but nothing more.

'You're eating?' he says.

I gesture to the remnants of a modest breakfast on the tray before me. 'First time since the op.'

He closes the door, then perches on the end of the bed. 'How're you doing?'

I take a moment to finish the juice before answering. It gives me time to coerce the jumbled thoughts going through my head into a coherent sentence.

'They moved me in here last night. I took a turn for the worse, and they figured the peace and quiet would do me good.'

'But, you're going to be all right?'

'I'm okay, in the circumstances. Even though—'

'If Simon wasn't dead, you would be.'

There. One of us has said it aloud.

I nod.

'Survivor's guilt,' says David, the certainty in his voice punching me in the chest with its brutal honesty.

'I haven't seen that listed on the diagnosis,' I reply, indicating the medical notes clipped to the board on the wall next to the door.

'Amateurs,' he says, and winks.

I wipe the tears tracking down my cheeks. 'Have the police spoken to you?'

The smile disappears from his face. 'After you'd been taken to hospital, yes. Just routine, I think. Why? Have they been here?'

'Yesterday. A police constable – a bloke, and a woman. She was senior to him. Forbes.'

'Ah, the attack dog. That's the one.'

We both smile at that, and then he turns serious once more.

'What did they ask you?'

'They wanted to know why we were there, who organised it, why I went.'

'What did you tell them?'

'Not a lot. I can't remember much of it, to be honest.' I place the empty cup on the tray, then nod my thanks to David as he scoops it off the bed and puts it on the table under the window.

He helps me ease back onto my pillows, then when I'm settled he moves to the chair.

I frown at the memory of the police questioning. 'She was very rude. Demanded to know how I'd managed to go out if my health was so bad.'

'Did you tell her you were a complete space cadet and medicated up to your eyeballs?'

'After I'd had a go at her about her attitude, yes. They left after the ward sister interrupted them to ask what was going on.'

David gives a low whistle through his teeth.

'Yeah. I know,' I sigh. 'But she pissed me off.'

He leans forward. 'What *do* you remember?'

It's something I've been asking myself since the two police officers left yesterday.

The clarity with which some of the day's events come back to me is muted by the gaps in my memory, and it scares me.

Not that I'll tell David about that.

Not yet.

Instead, I clear my throat.

'I remember Bec picking me up from Mum and Dad's. She was late – it was the first time she'd been there, because she usually collected me from the flat if we were going out anywhere and it was her turn to drive.'

We don't mention the fact that I had to sell my flat once my health deteriorated to the point where I couldn't care for myself.

'You looked really pale. I was worried,' says David.

'Mum was fussing – she was concerned I wasn't wearing enough clothes and that I'd catch a cold, even though I looked like—'

'An Eskimo.'

I reach out for his hand. 'I'll be honest, I felt like shit, but you'd all organised it and I didn't want to let you down.'

'You could've said something. We could've cancelled.'

I squeeze his fingers and let go. 'But it was meant to be our last time together. I couldn't cancel that. Besides, I'd taken extra painkillers.'

His brow furrows. 'Was that wise? I mean, those things could floor a horse.'

'I just wanted to enjoy myself,' I say in a small voice.

I won't admit it, but he's got me worried now.

Because maybe I shouldn't have taken the extra

dosage. David's got a point about the strength of the medication I was on.

I recall being given the first tentative prescription by Doctor Ashwan, the lecture that accompanied it, and the fact that when I got back home to Mum and Dad's I tore up the instructions into tiny pieces before flushing them down the toilet because I was too afraid to read them.

'Lisa?'

David is watching me, and I realise I've been silent for too long.

'I remember Hayley being excited.'

He rolls his eyes. 'If Forbes is a Rottweiler, then Hayley is a Yorkshire Terrier.'

We laugh, and the tension leaves the room for a moment.

'We won the first game, didn't we?' I say.

'We did. Beat the record by fifteen seconds, which is why we took the next challenge. The haunted house. I got the impression you were struggling by then.'

'I was.'

I'm not kidding. If it hadn't been for Simon's insistence that we continue to play, and his derisory remark about making memories – he meant well, but it sounded callous coming from him of all people – then I'd never have agreed to it.

'What do you remember about that?' says David.

'Not much. I think Hayley was helping me along by that point. I felt woozy.'

'The painkillers?'

'Must have been. Plus, all those flashing lights and special effects. It was disorientating.'

'It was meant to be. They don't want you to have an easy win.'

'I realise that.' I'm not cross with him, but he does have a way of stating the obvious sometimes. I don't berate him, but instead point to the water jug on the dresser and he obliges by filling a glass and passing it to me.

I gulp half, then exhale. 'I remember the lights going out. Hayley let go of my arm, and I lost my sense of direction. Simon laughed because she screamed, and then I tripped over something. I heard you saying they should switch the lights on, and then it all went quiet. I couldn't hear anything except my own breathing. I panicked. I thought you'd all left me. I called out, but no one answered. I – I can't remember anything after that.'

'I don't remember you calling out,' said David.

'Are you sure the drugs weren't making you hallucinate?'

'I'm sure.'

But then I pause.

Am I?

8

HAYLEY

Her name is Harriet Roxburgh, and according to the internet search I typed in yesterday after she called, she's the youngest daughter of a business mogul who keeps his offices in Canary Wharf and owns property in Mayfair.

Her husband is a distant nephew of a minor royal, and it's estimated that their wedding eight years ago cost well in excess of six figures, which goes some way to explain why the house is on a prestigious spit of land overlooking a marina.

I'm not surprised. She sounds like the sort of woman who should have a title in front of her name. A Lady, or an Honourable. Something like that.

I'm taken aback when she answers the solid oak

front door to the five-bedroom detached house in jeans and a long-sleeved T-shirt, because she looks like neither of those. She's older than I imagined – perhaps late thirties – and has a red-faced toddler balanced on her hip.

'Sorry,' she says in a clipped, practised voice that manages to hide almost all but the subtlest of Geordie accents. 'I was on the phone to my mother-in-law.'

She rolls her eyes for emphasis as she steps aside to let me over the threshold, pushing her light-brown hair out of her eyes.

I'm immediately aware of the sweet scent of furniture polish wafting through the airy light space I've walked into.

It's not a hallway – it's too wide for that. It's more like an atrium, and as I raise my gaze I'm astounded to see criss-crossing beams that intersect this part of the house. Above and in front of me there's a balcony, and I'm sure I can spot the soft furnishings of a bedroom beyond.

Stairs lead up from my right and sweep across the hallway under the balcony and off to a mezzanine level from which the soft sound of classical music emanates. It's all strings and cellos and sweeping sonatas.

The door swishes closed behind me, and Harriet shifts the kid from one hip to the other. 'I suppose all of your clients have a clean around before you turn up.'

I smile, as she expects me to, and then utter the words that I used to rehearse and now spew out on autopilot. 'Not all of them are as fastidious about their cleaning as this. Your home is wonderful.'

Her shoulders relax as she breaks into a grin. 'Do you have kids?'

Fuck, no. Perish the thought.

'Actually, no. I find my nieces enough of a handful.'

'Ah.' She jiggles the toddler, who looks like he might throw up. 'This one here was a complete surprise. I didn't expect to start late in life. How do you normally do this? Should I show you around first?'

'That's a good idea. That way I can get my bearings, and then we can discuss what services my company offers that will help you achieve a more balanced lifestyle.'

I follow her through the hallway into a living room with the most enormous television I've ever seen bolted to one wall, and then to a bespoke kitchen that looks as if it cost as much as the wedding, and then upstairs to ooh and aah at the lavish interior design and strategically placed soft furnishings.

All the time, the brat on her arm is whining, fidgeting, his gaze moving from his mother to me to see if his antics will get the attention he wants because the focus – for now – isn't on him.

I ignore him. I'm too in awe of my surroundings to be bothered with a snivelling kid.

By the time Harriet's mobile phone rings, interrupting her monotonous commentary about the way the skylights in the house were angled to catch just the right amount of sunshine in the mornings and evenings, it's all I can do to batten down the envy that is coursing through me.

Instead, I smile politely as she turns away. I move towards the floor-to-ceiling window in here, the upper lounge room according to the potential client.

'I'm sorry – this is going to take a moment,' she says, jiggling the kid who's stopped looking sick and now appears ready to throw the tantrum to end all tantrums. 'I'll be right back.'

I hold up a hand to let her know that's fine with me – as if I have a choice – and turn away.

Beyond the glass, beyond the masts in the

marina, I can see the edges of Southampton city centre, the trees that form a perimeter around the Common.

A shiver crawls down my neck and across my shoulders.

I turn away from the view and run my gaze over the trinkets and curios that have been dotted across the surface of a baby grand piano. I wander over and run my fingers over the lid that hides the keys, then sniff the air.

She has polished all of this as well, and as I peer under the lid at the dusty keys I wonder how often the instrument is actually played, and how much of its presence here is for show.

Perhaps one day the snivelling brat will be forced to have piano lessons; a final justification for the exuberance of having the piano in the first place.

I can still hear her in the other room. A floorboard creaks as she paces back and forth. Whatever the conversation, it sounds like she's going to be a while yet.

I sigh and check my watch.

The hospital's visiting times have another two hours to go, but I've got no intention of seeing Lisa there again.

Once was enough.

I don't want to bump into the police. I mean, they're going to go there, aren't they?

They'll want to speak to her, like they spoke to me the morning after Simon died.

I couldn't believe it when they turned up at my front door.

Two of them: a woman, whose chin jutted out the moment I swung the door open as if she was ready to pounce, and a younger man in uniform who looked terrified to find himself within fifty feet of her.

She barked a string of words starting with her rank and name and, after inviting herself in, spent the next twenty minutes grilling me about what went on in the escape room.

What did she expect went on in a bloody escape room? We were trying to escape, I told her; that was the whole point.

Her colleague smirked at my answer and for a moment I thought I'd scored a point there, but then the woman – Forbes, that's her – glared at me. We went over and over the same things, and for a moment I wondered if I was talking nonsense before I realised what she was trying to do.

She was trying to trip me up, see if I made a

mistake in my retelling of what we did, where we went, what happened.

I was shaking by the time they left. I hated the way she left me exposed, questioning my own recollection, and worrying if I'd said too much – or too little.

I square my shoulders and move across the thick carpet to a bookshelf where Harriet has arranged matching photograph frames.

There are the obligatory pre- and post-birth studio photographs, perfect poses belying the sleepless nights and crappy nappies that surely followed the glamorous pregnancy. Next to these are older images showing the smiling couple – I'm presuming that's her husband – holding up glasses of frothing beer, ski goggles on their heads; canoeing along a river somewhere green and lush and definitely not anywhere near Southampton; and then—

I stop.

The last photograph shows a younger Harriet and the same man amongst a group of friends all piled onto a too-small sofa and holding champagne flutes in their hands. In the other hand, each of them is holding a certificate.

A graduation certificate.

I put the photograph down before I drop it and turn away, my mouth dry.

From the other room, the kid screams in frustration, driving needles into my already frayed nerves.

The photograph has brought back the wrong memories, and now that they swirl around in my head, I know I won't sleep tonight.

Because it reminds me too much of my own university days.

With the others.

With him.

And then, without him.

Because, for a brief spell in that first year, there were six of us.

Not five.

9

DAVID

THE NARROW STREET is lined with cars, delivery vans and school mums in hulking four-by-four vehicles too big for them to handle. A cacophony of engines, car horns and frustrated shouting fills the air.

Half past three on a Wednesday afternoon; school's out; bedlam.

The pavements of this 1950s-created urban sprawl are too narrow, too uneven, too cluttered with café blackboards, buskers, and pensioners who congregate in the middle of the path to chat with someone they only saw yesterday but might have missed some gossip in the meantime.

They stand, oblivious to people who split like river tributaries around them, such is their eagerness to pass the time of day repeating the news rather than go home to an empty room to stare at the walls, alone.

Kids in brightly coloured uniforms fill the pavements, swarming in and out of shops, dumping their backpacks and sports bags in the doorways, ignorant of the assault course they're leaving in the way for other customers to navigate through.

I shove my way past a group of four teenage girls, ignore their mocking sniggers at my cycling gear, and open a refrigerator door. Goosebumps cover my forearms as I reach towards the back of the shelf and wrap my fingers around the last can of energy drink.

No wonder the kids are screaming and shouting at decibels that would make a death metal band's eyes water. They're all sky-high on caffeine and sugar.

I let the refrigerator door slam shut and elbow my way to the counter, where Mr Khoury is doing his best to stop the next barrage of kids coming in before he's had a chance to make sure the ones leaving haven't nicked half his stock.

We share a weary glance as he applies a bony finger to the button on the till, and then I hand over some coins.

'Put the change in the charity tin,' I say, and wonder which of the coloured cans on the counter will benefit.

Probably the local cat shelter. It's the one that's the most faded, the most scratched and dented.

Mr Khoury smiles and holds up the fifty pence piece. 'Well, it must be the Kidney Foundation, no?'

My gaze falls to the tin next to the one with white kittens plastered across the front of it and I wonder why I hadn't noticed it before.

'It's new,' says Khoury before I can ask. 'The daughter of one of my regulars has had a very successful operation this past week. It's a good cause, isn't it? Very good cause.'

Except I can't hear him anymore because I'm at the door, climbing over bags and trying not to lose my footing as my cleated shoes try to slide out from under me. I shove the can of drink down the front of my jersey and grasp the doorframe with gloved hands, then lurch forwards onto the pavement.

I'm panting, but not from exertion.

I reach my carbon-framed bike and breathe a sigh of relief. Both wheels are still attached, and the paintwork is immaculate.

I loop the helmet straps over the handlebar and

pop open the can. It's half empty within seconds, and a belch erupts before I've got time to blink.

A pensioner scuttles past with a disapproving expression, her mouth turned downwards.

I mutter an apology, embarrassed because my own grandmother would've glared at me the same way, and then glance back towards the convenience shop.

It's one of those "early morning through to late at night" businesses. God knows when Khoury and his other half sleep, because one of them is always present, either manning the till, restocking the shelves or standing in the doorway smiling and passing the time of day with anyone who stops to chat.

It's a good three miles away from Lisa's parents' house though, so what are the chances that her mum shops there? What are the chances Mrs Ashton – Judy – drives all the way over here on a regular basis? What are the chances Mr Khoury was talking about someone else entirely when he dropped my change into the charity tin next to his till?

But the thought is now crawling through my brain, tiptoeing over synapses and slowly curating a paranoia that I know won't leave me.

Not now it's woven its way into my consciousness.

I tip back my head and finish the drink before tossing the can into a recycling bin bolted to a nearby lamp post, and unlock the bike. I place the helmet on my head, clip the chin strap into place and then push the bike to the kerb. A bus shoots past, the driver intent on the road in front of him as he accelerates away. I push off and clip my shoes to my pedals, making the most of the drag from the vehicle in front.

After half a mile of weaving between cars, pedestrians and slower cyclists, I bump the bike up the kerb and join a cycle path the council created a couple of years ago.

I slow, not for safety but because the winding route takes me along a narrow tree-lined space that always provides a respite from the concrete world over my shoulder after a day's work. I've found it counteracts some of the stress, and I'm hoping to hell it helps now, despite the bare branches above and mottled leaves that cover the path.

A blackbird emits a sharp retort before skimming across the path in front of me, angling its wings to land at the foot of a fir tree, the canopy shading us both from the weak afternoon sun.

A shiver crosses my shoulders, and I change gears, picking up speed as I shoot out the other side of the woodland and on to a straight stretch that runs parallel to the train tracks.

The faded yellow front end of a train appears in the distance, barrelling towards me. I recognise it as one of the three-carriage ones like I used to catch into work before I took up cycling.

As it swoops past, I catch a glimpse of the passengers' faces – pale blurs at windows. Some peer at the cycling track, others are bowed, perhaps squinting at laptops or a last futile attempt at the morning's crossword before home, where they can switch on the evening news and shout at the screen, at the injustices in the world, at all the unfairness and death.

I grit my teeth and push down on the pedals, forcing another sprint until the pain in my calf muscles threatens cramp.

I recall a throwaway comment one of my lecturers spouted as we were hustling out of the room one summer's day at university all those years ago, and I brake hard.

There's a muttered curse from behind, and an overweight man in his fifties wobbles past on a mountain bike a size too small for his frame.

I hold up my hand to say sorry, but he's already turning the corner of the cycle path. Another moment, and he's out of sight.

The words are still going around in my head though.

Nothing is more wretched than the mind of a man conscious of guilt.

10

LISA

IF IT WASN'T for the throbbing ache in my side, I swear I'd be out the door by now.

I was never any good at doing nothing, and four days post-operation, I'm getting frustrated and bored. I need something to do.

They moved me back to the main ward this morning. Something about needing the room for someone else.

I miss the privacy.

I've read the gossip magazines Mum brought in from cover to cover despite the flaky fakery within the glossy pages, tried the hospital radio station, and attempted to read a book.

And still the woman in the bed opposite me is trying to engage me in conversation.

I need to get out of here.

I will my body to heal, to mend itself, to accept the gift it's been given. A last-minute reprieve from pain, and eventual death.

I exhale, lie back, and stare at the ceiling tiles, my thoughts returning to my donor.

Of course, none of us are going to admit it to each other now, but Simon could be a right bastard.

I chew my lip.

It was almost comical, the way you could be chatting away to him and then he'd turn to you with a blank expression.

'Hmm?' he'd say, and raise his eyebrows.

Sometimes he'd give a slight shake of his head and lean towards you, as if incredulous that you'd dare interrupt him. Usually it was from watching whatever drivel was on the nearest television, even if you were in a pub and the adverts were on at half-time.

It was almost comical, but mostly infuriating, especially when you realised this was his default position. It wasn't that he couldn't hear you; he simply couldn't care less about what you were saying to him.

He did it to me one final time, three weeks ago.

I was desperate by then.

Bec, Hayley, David and Simon had all had blood tests at the same time in an attempt to try to help me.

Except when the results came through, only one of them was a match.

A perfect match.

I didn't want to ask him, but the conversation with my specialist the day before had convinced me I no longer had a choice.

I was going to die, and Simon was the only hope I had of surviving.

At least, his kidney was.

'Hmm?'

I fought down the urge to erupt with anger – or succumb to the tears of frustration and fear that were threatening.

Couldn't he see this was important? That my life depended on him?

'They gave me some brochures to explain it all, look.'

I'd shoved them across the pine kitchen table at him, the rough surface catching on the edge of one of the pages and turning it off-kilter.

Simon pushed his glasses up his nose before he peered at the glossy offerings, his mouth twisting in disdain.

'They have brochures for this?'

'I guess it helps explain things better for living donors.'

'Helps … right.' He sighed and cocked an eyebrow as he opened out one of the leaflets.

I tried to remember when the man I'd spent my final teenage years with had turned into such a cruel person.

Had he always been like this?

I'd never seen him physically strike anyone, not even the boys who tried to rile him during those early days at grammar school. After a while they seemed to sense that he wouldn't stoop to their level of one-upmanship and simply ignored him. As we got older and ended up at the same university, he wouldn't even contemplate entering a pub if there was the slightest chance that something might kick off.

No, Simon's strength was in what he said. Or, more to the point, what he didn't say.

He didn't demand things from people, but he wouldn't say "please" or "thank you" afterwards, either. He simply expected everyone to bend to his will.

Why did we all go along with it?

Maybe it was because we wanted to keep our

group together. To not be the first person to raise their voice against him in case it destroyed all our friendships.

Maybe it was because he knew things.

About us.

He knew things about me, that was for sure. Things I never wanted the others to find out in case they ostracised me from the group.

If he wanted to. If he felt like it.

I didn't have any other friends; the thought of socialising with anyone else terrified me. I'd become used to hanging around with the same people for over seven years.

How was I supposed to start again on top of everything else I'd been going through?

The thought terrified me.

'Do you want a hot drink?' I'd asked him.

'Go on, then.'

I turned away from him, busying myself with making tea – Earl Grey, and none of that supermarket own-brand shit, otherwise he'd never let me hear the end of it.

The chair scraped across the tiled floor, and then he began to pace, flicking through one brochure at a time before it landed back on the table, creating an untidy heap.

I swallowed, and concentrated on squashing the teabag against the side of his cup, trying to get the colour of the water to some sort of acceptable tint before adding a splash of semi-skimmed milk.

The bergamot aroma filled the tiny space, reminding me of summer afternoons and cake frosting at my grandmother's house, and I fought down the rising panic in my chest as a familiar sound reached me.

He'd returned to the chair, his shoe tapping the floor. He was bouncing one leg up and down as he concentrated, a tic he'd had since our first mock exams all those years ago. It was when I'd first noticed how anxious he was under the surface, and how hard he worked to keep that anxiety hidden.

It was why he so often lashed out with his words – to hide his own fears, I suppose.

I was making excuses for him again.

I turned away from the kitchen worktop and took the two mugs of tea over to where he sat, placing one before him and taking a seat opposite.

He didn't say anything. Didn't look up to acknowledge me. Didn't thank me for the tea, of course.

After five more minutes, I couldn't stand the silence any longer.

'What do you think?'

He shook his head, pushed away the mug of tea and rose from his chair, abandoning the leaflets now strewn over the table.

'I've changed my mind. I'm not doing it, Lisa.'

He didn't even apologise before walking out the door.

11

LISA

THEY DON'T KNOW.

I haven't told my parents about that last conversation with Simon, so when they come to see me at visiting time the next day, I force it to the back of my mind.

They never knew he was a match. They never knew he'd denied me the chance to live.

Right now, in death, he's their knight in shining armour and I don't want to spoil the illusion for them.

What would I say? Guess what – Simon signed my death warrant?

Of course, there's also a grim satisfaction lurking at the back of my mind, one I daren't voice out loud.

That I'm alive because of him.

I sense their presence before they appear; a slight change in the air followed by voices out in the corridor. They are smiling as they enter the ward, and any worries I've been hoarding are forgotten as I see their faces.

Mum stands at the side of the bed and appraises me. 'Well. Here we are. On the mend at last.'

Her relief is palpable, and she sinks into the chair Dad pulls over for her with a sigh.

'Have you spoken to them?'

'Who?' says Mum.

'Simon's parents.'

She fusses with the small handbag in her lap.

Dad runs a hand through thinning close-cropped hair. 'We haven't. The specialist team are going to organise a session early next week for you to meet with them. Given that you shouldn't have known who your donor was, I think they're in damage control. We didn't know what else to do, so we agreed to it …'

His voice drifts off as his hand drops away, and his gaze slides to the tiled floor.

'We wouldn't know what to say to his mum and

dad, anyway,' says Mum. 'Not in the circumstances. Not with the police—'

'Have they spoken to you? The police?'

'The day before yesterday. After we came to see you.'

'Why? What did they say?'

'I suppose because of where he died they have to look into things.'

'What things?'

'It's all right, love.' Dad has picked up on the note of panic in my voice and leans forward. 'It's probably routine enquiries, as they call it. Because Simon died out of the blue. He didn't have any health issues, did he?'

I shake my head. 'Not that I knew about.'

'Well, there you go then. I expect the coroner wants to dot the I's and cross the T's.'

I try not to snort with bitter laughter. Dad's fondness for television crime shows means he's suddenly become a leading expert in police investigations.

He has a point, though.

They'll want to know. They'll find out eventually.

'They say he was in trouble, financially.' Mum lowers her voice after glancing over her shoulder.

There's no one listening in, but I feel the temperature drop a few degrees regardless.

'Was he?'

This is news to me.

Simon was the one who sneered at Hayley's frivolous clothing purchases, at David's inability to save twenty per cent of his salary every month towards his house deposit, at Bec's habit of chiding people for paying back money she'd only recently let them borrow.

And he hated the fact that I bought my flat while he rented a one-bedroom loft apartment near the train station, almost as if it were a competition to get on the property ladder and he'd lost.

'How do you know?' I say. 'Who said he was?'

Mum shrugs; her default position when she's been caught gossiping. 'A few people.'

'Who?'

'Brenda, who works at the same IT company Simon used to. You know – the woman I go to choir with on Thursday nights. She said he left there because he said it didn't pay enough.'

'Mum, loads of people leave jobs to get something that pays better.'

'They're one of the top employers around here. And, Brenda said there was a rumour going around that he had a gambling habit, and that he got fired. He didn't quit.'

'Really?'

She's got my attention now.

'In what way?'

'She didn't know – it was just something she'd heard. Where did he end up working after that?'

'He told me he was freelancing.'

'So, he was unemployed?'

'No, Mum. He was juggling a few contracts – and doing quite well out of it, he said.'

I fall silent, shocked by the news.

What else didn't I know about Simon?

12

DAVID

WHY AN ESCAPE ROOM?

Because it was a distraction – in more ways than one.

I rub at my tired, scratchy eyes before flicking on the kettle and shoving a heaped teaspoon of instant coffee into a chipped mug.

When I open the refrigerator, I groan. I forgot to buy milk on the way home yesterday, and there's no time to walk to the petrol station at the end of the next street to buy some – not if I'm going to get to work on time.

I check my watch, then glare at the kettle as steam shoots from the spout. I'll just have to add an extra spoonful of sugar and be done with it.

As I take my coffee through to the living room, I

spot the council tax bill on the small dining table that doubles as a makeshift desk. I was meant to pay it on Monday, but with everything else that has happened these past six days, I'd forgotten that, too. I keep meaning to set it up as a standing order, but haven't got around to it. Again.

I put the coffee mug on an upturned sales brochure for double glazing that hasn't yet found its way to the recycling bin, pull my mobile from my trouser pocket and log into the banking app.

I hate being late paying bills. I pride myself on being organised, on being dependable. It's why the others rely on me – they know I won't let them down.

That done, I take a sip of coffee and close my eyes as the first caffeine hit smacks my gums. It's not as satisfying as the real thing, of course.

I blink, and try to decide whether to take the contact lenses out and wear my glasses instead. When I peer through the slats of the blinds that screen the back window, I change my mind.

It's pissing down with rain, and I can't stand cycling wearing glasses when it's like this – with the glasses fogging up and covered in raindrops, it's too disorientating. Dangerous too, given the amount of traffic at this time of day.

I wander over to where I dumped my backpack on the armchair when I came downstairs and check the side pocket. The bottle of eye drops is inside, and there is plenty to keep me going today.

I frown as my fingers find thick paper, the surface shiny under my touch.

Giving it a tug, I emit a surprised grunt when I recognise the bright colours of the escape room company's logo, the glossy surface of the brochure taken up with photographs.

These are evidently posed by actors – or the owners' friends; the fixed smiles, furrowed brows or exasperated expressions are too staged, too fake.

Still, it convinced Lisa and the others.

It was, after all, one of the few activities anyone in the group had suggested that Lisa would actually be capable of taking part in, given the fragile state of her health.

Simon, of course, had rolled his eyes and said escape rooms were pathetic and that no doubt we'd complete the three rooms on offer in record time. He even went so far as to suggest that the organisers knew their "fun group activity" wouldn't tax our grey matter too much, hence the forty per cent group discount they offered on the back of the brochure. Just some people who were taking advantage of the latest trend, who wouldn't be around in a year's time.

Hayley and Bec had come to my rescue, Bec at least having the sense to point out to her ex-fiancé that given all of our current plans to save our money, none of the other options under consideration for Lisa's birthday were appropriate — or viable.

Simon had glared at her then, and sulked for the rest of the evening. When I left to help Lisa into Bec's car to get a lift home, she and Simon still weren't talking.

At least the day we arrived at the escape room, he'd perked up after a couple of drinks beforehand at a bar over the road.

For a brief moment, I saw a flash of the old candour in Simon. The same mischievous lad who'd charmed me when I'd first met him at university because he'd been more daring, and the same determined expression that had ensured our secret had been kept safe for so long.

Even he had to admit the first escape room was fun — and it was.

Corny, yes, but exactly what we all needed, especially with Lisa's health clearly deteriorating within the space of the week since we'd last seen her.

Her skin was translucent; an unhealthy paleness that glowed eerily under the special effects lighting.

'Maybe we should cancel,' I said as we were about to start.

She reached out and squeezed my hand. 'No, don't. It'll be okay.'

I nodded, happy to grant her wish and then turned my attention to the challenge we'd been set.

The first room had been decorated to look as if it were a modern office, with six laptop computer screens flickering on different desks and a blue hue to the lighting. We stood in the middle of the room after the door closed behind us, and I was about to voice my disappointment, when a countdown was beamed in bright red numbers on one of the walls.

Sixty minutes.

Sixty minutes, until what?

That became apparent as one of the laptop screens changed and a pre-recording of a man in a scientist's white overcoat began speaking. A terrorist cell had stolen the secret formula for a bioweapon – and our team was tasked with tracking down the suspects and stopping the bomb from being detonated. We would escape when our instructions typed into each laptop resulted in the correct combination of answers.

In sixty minutes?

Eat your heart out, Jack Bauer.

I turned to see Simon leaning against the wall, his pupils dilated, and bit back a sigh. Instead, I called him over.

'Come on, Simon. Computers and linear thinking are your areas of expertise. Any ideas?'

I tried, really, I did. I wanted it to be a special day; I wanted it to be like it was in that first term at university – the five of us determined to succeed.

There was no way we were going to fail the first game, we'd promised ourselves that much.

By the time we were thirty minutes in, though, I realised he was the worse for wear, talking too loudly and bumping into one of the desks, sending a laptop crashing to the floor.

I nodded to Hayley, and she pulled out a bottle of water from her tote bag, handing it to Simon with a suggestion he drink it.

'I think those Manhattans you had in the bar over the road went to your head,' she said, and then laughed to take the edge off her words.

Mutely, Simon uncapped the bottle and drained the contents before wiping his mouth with the back of his hand. 'Right. Let's get out of here.'

We were on the cusp of cracking the final clue to escape from the first room when I turned to Lisa to share our relief at our success.

She staggered, only stopping herself from tumbling to the ground by throwing her hand out and finding the wall.

I hurried over to her, putting my hand on her shoulder, but she shook her head.

'I'm all right.'

'She's pissed,' said Simon, and cackled. 'Guess you shouldn't have tried my cocktail with the meds you're on.'

'Oh, shut up,' Bec snapped at him. She turned her attention to the panel in front of her and tapped in the sequence we'd just agreed.

I heard the locking mechanism give way, and then the exit door opened, revealing itself behind a filing cabinet we'd been rifling through for clues only twenty minutes before.

Piped music blared from hidden speakers – a fanfare that sounded like a bad home recording, or a cheap download.

That lifted the mood, and Simon's harsh words

were forgotten for a moment as we high-fived each other.

Even Lisa was smiling at that point, but I noticed how she relied on Hayley for support and trailed along behind the rest of us as we made our way along the corridor to the next escape room.

As soon as the door swung shut behind us, I knew we were in trouble.

Simon was slurring his words, needling Bec as she read out the first set of instructions.

I ignored him and turned in a circle, taking in our new surroundings.

A haunted house wasn't original, but it did provide a different challenge to the espionage one we'd completed. Fake cobwebs clung to the ceiling, and I watched as Bec eyed an enormous furry spider in one corner with alarm. She caught me looking, and forced a smile.

'Let's not hang around too long in here, all right?'

Then the lights went out, and everything changed.

It took me a moment to fight the sudden disorientating darkness and realise that the screaming I could hear wasn't pre-recorded at all.

It was Hayley.

13

HAYLEY

MY SPIRITS LIFT the moment the glass doors to the shopping centre swish open, and I hitch my handbag up my shoulder.

I stride towards the escalator, relaxing once I place my hand on the rubber handrail and lift my gaze to the pretty lights that hang from the glass ceiling.

A pale blue sky peers through, and I'm thankful for the winter sun warming the inside of my car that's parked on the roof of the multi-storey opposite, awaiting my return.

This is my natural environment.

Not the hospital.

Above me, men and women bustle past the gleaming aluminium railings either side of the escalators clutching their latest purchases, laden with branded shopping bags while holding phones to their ears. They weave amongst each other like pigeons, homing in on the next item on their lists of must-haves and wants.

Bec says she gets disoriented in shopping centres. Too many people, too many different sounds, big and brash window displays that demand to be noticed, pushy salesmen and women.

Not me.

I smile while I survey the floor below and the escalator takes me higher.

Down there are all the cheap shops, the ones that have the latest Top Ten hits, the music blaring at high volume, competing with the stores next door.

Every shop down there has white security alarm posts and someone actively checking bags before customers are allowed to leave the store.

Which is ironic, because down there the buy-one-get-one-free brigade hang around to seek out the cheaper clothing, the discounted shoes and souvenirs that only cost a quid or two. After that, they stuff their faces with grease and fat at the sprawling food court.

I've worked hard so I don't have to shop down there.

I reach the next level and cast my gaze across the mezzanine, taking in the jewellery counters that glisten through plate-glass windows and the travel agents' signs offering exclusive river cruises and guided safaris for the discerning adventurer.

I wonder if I should go away.

There's part of me that wants to run, and never stop. Never come back.

The thought leaves me melancholy, a clear sign that I should treat myself, be kinder to myself – that's what the self-help books in the window display of the bookshop I pass tell me, at least.

Further on, plush sofas and armchairs have been arranged around an ornate display of ferns in such a way as to allow the people who rest here a modicum of privacy as they pause for a moment between purchases.

The music here is different, too – instead of the brash pop beats of the lower level, here classical music is piped through hidden speakers, a string quartet that encourages people to stay, take their time, and spend more.

I peer over the nearest palm fronds and spot a

woman in a grey business suit and pearls, her hair swept up into a chignon as she rustles a copy of the financial newspaper in her hands, her attention taken fully by her reading material. She doesn't look up; doesn't seem to care what is going on around her, or what people think of her.

I envy her confidence.

I set my sights on the large department store off to the right. They don't know me here, and I'm elated that I can move around in anonymity.

Here too, classical music plays unobtrusively. Shoppers are encouraged to meander, browse, and use credit cards with the word "platinum" embossed across the front.

I start to relax, inhaling the heady scents of sandalwood and musk as I glide past the perfume displays, and smile at the assistant who stands chatting next to a burly security guard in a smart uniform, his arms across his chest as he laughs with the woman and teases her while she works.

Through an archway, I spot the department store's homewares department and sigh at the thought of the plush throws, cushions and other soft fabrics that I'd love to get, but can't.

Not today.

I move past the archway and set my sights on the middle of the store, weaving my way between handbags and umbrellas.

I finally reach the boutique displays of women's clothing and pluck a hanger from the rail, running my eyes down the dress as I touch the smooth satin fabric.

Two other women browse the rails, but we don't make eye contact. We don't smile at each other. It's as if there's an unspoken rule in here that we don't need each other's approval. We don't need to explain why we shop in here rather than down there.

I pause when I spot the price tag deftly pinned to the designer label, check over my shoulder and then put it back.

Neither of them look up. Neither of them see me decide that I can't afford that today.

I move away from the clothing rails, back to the tiled floor that meanders around the department store, a concrete river that takes me past row upon row of displays: shoes, leather belts, purses.

I slow my pace as I approach the racks of make-up, pausing to gawp at the endless shades of eyeshadow, blush, and mascara. I need another lipstick, but not today.

Today I want something extra special, to cheer me up. To help me recover from the trauma of the past few days.

I shouldn't, but I will.

___

14

LISA

The stench hits me first.

An overpowering aroma of too many flowers, too much pollen, and a mixture of fragrances that hit my senses the minute Mum opens the front door and stands to one side to let me pass.

'I'm going to—'

I sneeze, and then I double up in pain.

I can't prevent the yelp that escapes, and suddenly Dad's there, clutching my arm for a moment before he takes off into the lounge. I can hear him opening the windows, despite the cold air that's blasting from the street outside.

'I told you it'd be too much for her allergies,' he calls out.

'It was the neighbours,' says Mum, wringing the

free newspaper between her hands. She drops it into the recycling basket at the bottom of the stairs where it lands every week, unread and unwanted. 'And your work colleagues. And everybody else. There are too many flowers, Lisa.'

'Throw them out,' I gasp. 'I don't want them.'

Mum pouts. 'The neighbours will see.'

Dad passes us with three vases in his grip, on his way through to the kitchen where no doubt there are more floral arrangements waiting to try and kill me.

I hear the back door open; the lid to the wheelie bin clangs shut, and he returns with a triumphant look in his eyes.

'All gone.'

Mum rolls her eyes. 'I'll put the kettle on.'

It's her answer to everything, but I'm too weak to argue and simply nod.

It's strange – yesterday at the hospital with the prospect of going home, I was excited. I'd sent texts to my ex-boss, Charlie, to tell him how I was doing, and, minutes after his response ("Great!"), I got a text from Beatrice, an older colleague, saying how Charlie was already mooting my return, even if it were only on a part-time basis to begin with.

Today, the cloying familiarity of Mum and Dad's house has sent it all crashing down again.

Simon is dead, I remind myself.

What the hell was I thinking, getting excited about going back to work?

Dad heads towards me, a wry smile on his face before he pats my arm and steers me towards the living room.

'Come on. Let's get you comfortable.'

'I don't feel too good, Dad. I feel faint.'

I can hear it in my voice; the uncertainty. The shock.

The horror.

How did Simon die?

'The doctors said you might. Over here. I'll wrap this blanket around you, okay?'

He shakes it out and holds it up expectantly as I shuffle across the thick carpet to his favourite chair.

I've been occupying it for the past three weeks, and he's never said a word. Now, he winks.

'At least I'll finally get my chair back.'

It does the trick. The corner of my mouth twitches and I settle back while he fusses around me.

'How are you now? A bit better?'

'A bit, thanks. I need my phone. Sorry, I left it in my bag.'

'I'll go and get it.'

He disappears for a moment, and then returns with my bag. My hand delves inside, wraps around my mobile phone.

Dad reaches behind the television and pulls out a phone charger he keeps for his own mobile, then plugs it in next to me. 'I'd imagine that's on its last legs.'

He's not wrong – the battery icon is showing only two per cent.

'Thanks.'

I unlock the home screen and frown. There are no missed calls, no text messages, nothing. I was hoping at least Hayley or Bec would've sent me a "welcome home" message.

I open the email app, my heart sinking as I read through the offers from online stores, invitations to take surveys, and a late note from a distant aunt the previous night wishing me well.

'Did you need anything else?' says Dad.

Just some answers, I think.

'No, thanks.'

'Good.' He straightens, then stands there, unsure what to do next.

I'm embarrassed for him. I've always got on well with my dad, but we're not what I would call close. He's been doing his best, though.

We're saved by Mum shoving the door open with her elbow, a laden tea tray in her hands that she plonks down on the coffee table next to the sofa.

She passes a mug to me, and the simple gesture shakes me.

I'm home.

'Has anyone called the landline?'

I'm desperate for information. Something to help me understand.

She shakes her head. 'They're probably giving you some space to settle in again.' She reaches out for a ginger biscuit and nibbles the edge.

I've only been back twenty minutes, and already I'm fidgeting.

I check the screen on my phone again.

No new notifications. No new messages. No emails.

Nothing. Not since I saw David two days ago.

It's as if my friends have abandoned me now that they know I'm okay, and I don't know what to do.

15

LISA

THE THEME TUNE to the evening news carries through the floorboards from the living room below and provides a ten-second warning that, soon, I'll hear my dad's exclamations of 'Rubbish!' and 'Idiot!'.

My old childhood bedroom has become a sanctuary for me now, when previously – before Simon died – it was a place to mourn my future and all the plans and dreams I'd relegated as lost causes.

I'm sitting on my old single bed, my back against the wall in lieu of a headboard that was never fixed to the frame, and I reach behind me to plump up the pillows.

My eyes don't leave the laptop screen.

For the past half an hour I've been scrolling through my timeline on an old social media account I set up ten years ago, mid-way through studying the A-levels that would guarantee a place at the university of my choice.

I wanted to stay in Southampton, of course.

I'd grown up here, knew my way around, and had the added benefit of not having to pay rent to my parents while studying in order to keep any debt at bay.

I couldn't imagine having to move to a different city to study, not like some of my contemporaries. I'd have been disorientated, out of my depth, and anxious.

Besides, Simon was applying for Southampton and it seemed natural at the time to follow him.

We'd only been going out a few months by then, and I smile at the photographs from that time as I scroll past. It's hard not to – both of us are wearing ridiculous clothes, thinking we were the cool kids, and I'd forgotten about the short, choppy hairstyle I'd favoured at the time.

You can see it in his eyes, though. A cruelness, as if he's weighing up who to taunt next.

The cracks didn't appear in our relationship

until late spring that year, and after that we didn't last much longer.

I began to find his sense of humour too immature, and by the time I'd sat my A-level exams, I realised he'd hold me back if I stayed with him. Despite his interest in me in that first art class, it transpired he had no interest at all in my art, and saw it as a frivolous pursuit.

'Computers, Lisa. Coding. That's the future. Not this.'

He had waved a hand across the paintings I'd included in my portfolio, his top lip curling.

I scroll back to find the photographs I'd posted of my paintings in my timeline. I'd uploaded them when we split up a few days after he'd made that comment. Everyone else loved my work, leaving me feeling vindicated. Notably, none of the reactions on that post are from him.

Instead, he retaliated by posting a photograph of him with his new girlfriend – Stacey Alexander – two days later.

He knew it would hurt, and, despite knowing he was only using her to get to me, I let it.

I keep scrolling.

They only lasted two and a half months, and

then he dumped her when she accepted a place at Durham University.

The photographs from that first term at Southampton are filled with group shots from visits to London art galleries for assignments, stupid memes and dodgy videos taken at concerts with mobile phone cameras that pixelated badly and recorded the music as a mush of sound.

How many gigs and festivals had I watched with my own eyes and not through a phone screen?

I squint at a photograph from early December of that year and enlarge the image.

There he is.

Six foot two, slightly long dark hair, blue eyes and such a broad Glaswegian accent that it had taken me a few days of being around him before I'd been able to understand what he was saying.

He'd laughed at that.

'Stupid bloody idiot!'

I roll my eyes. Dad is in his element downstairs, and Mum will be in her armchair, tutting and offering her own commentary as the news stories progress from the tragic to the mediocre.

I tap the arrow key and scroll upwards, glancing at the date.

A few months after that last photograph was taken, I abandoned my social media account.

We all did.

I think it was David who'd suggested it, saying it was childish, that we didn't need to tell everyone else about everything we got up to, that we didn't need the validation.

Of course, some of our wider circle of acquaintances had laughed and said we'd be using it again within weeks, that we'd feel like we were missing out.

But they were wrong. We never did.

I shuffle on the duvet; my neck is sore from looking at the screen. Soon, my shoulders will ache but I need to know. I need to—

I find another photograph of him.

The photo is from a Christmas party – David is there, wearing a Santa hat and with his arm draped across Hayley's shoulders. She's smiling at the photographer – Bec, I presume, because I can't see her – and pointing at the felt reindeer antlers she's wearing as a hairband.

I smile. Only Hayley could make fake reindeer antlers look fashionable.

The Glaswegian is standing beside me, holding two fingers up behind my head like bunny ears.

We're all tagged here: at the top of the post it says Lisa Ashton plus six others.

I click to expand the list.

Greg Fisher. That's him.

Brash, bold, with a wicked sense of humour.

And too trusting.

16

LISA

THE DOORBELL RINGS the next day as Mum's wrapping a bright-yellow scarf around her neck, about to dash out to the red hatchback that's idling at the kerb.

The car is a make and model I can't recall the name of but looks dated already, even though I know it's only five years old.

Nine-thirty in the morning, and it's time for Mum's regular Saturday morning shopping trip with her friend, Barbara. A quick dash around the supermarket before Dad gets home from fishing, and then lunch. Regular as clockwork.

I crane my neck from my position in Dad's armchair, but I can't see the front step from here.

Dropping the television guide onto the coffee

table, I hold my breath to listen and then get the shock of my life.

Barbara's still sitting in the car. It's someone else at the door.

'Rebecca!'

Mum's delight at Bec's appearance is accompanied by an underlying note of grief and guilt, and Bec's voice has a forced cheeriness to it, its normal brightness sharpened to a brittle edge.

'I would've called, but—'

'No, no. She's in the living room. Go on through.'

'Is that okay? Are you on your way out?'

'Yes.' She raises her voice. 'I'll only be gone half an hour, Lisa. I've got my mobile on me if you need me in an emergency.'

And with that, the door slams and I see Mum's retreating figure hurrying down the front path towards the car.

She turns and gives the living room window a cheery wave before sliding into the passenger seat, and then they're off.

Thelma and Louise.

I'm still wearing a faint smile as the door to the living room opens and Bec peers in, her brow contorted with worry.

She's pale, and the scant make-up I can see appears old and worn away. She's been biting her bottom lip, and the skin is dry and ragged.

'Lisa?' Her shoulders are tense. 'Are you all right?'

'I've been better. Come on in.'

She shuffles forwards, a reluctance in her step before she moves across the carpet and perches on the arm of the sofa, as far away from me as she can get.

Her black leather handbag drops to the floor but she keeps hold of the strap, running it back and forth between her thumb and forefinger.

I swear under my breath. I've been so focused on my own trauma, I haven't considered what Bec must be going through, and I feel like the worst friend in the world for it.

'I'm so sorry,' I say. 'I know you'd split up with Simon, but this… this is just—'

'Thanks. The whole thing is pretty shit.' Bec's bottom lip trembles before she exhales, and it's only then that she raises her gaze to mine. 'You got home yesterday, yes?'

'Yes. As soon as they could see I was moving around better, and that the kidney and meds were all working as they should be, they discharged me.'

'What happens next? I mean, do you have to watch your diet and stuff?'

I swallow. It's painful to see her trying to make conversation when she's grieving, but I play along.

'Yes.' I gesture to all the pamphlets and A4-sized pages that are poking out from under the television guide on the coffee table. 'They've given me heaps of information, recipes, things like that. I have to record everything I eat and drink, and I have to go back three times a week for check-ups for the first month.'

'Wow. That's a lot.'

The carriage clock that Dad inherited from his aunt ticks away in the background from its position on the sideboard, another relic from the seventies that neither he nor Mum have the heart to part with and so it adds to the clutter at one end of the living room. It's deafening in the silence between us as we search for something else to say.

'I thought you might have come to the hospital to see me,' I say. 'I wanted to tell you how sorry I was.'

She sighs, her shoulders slumping before she hooks a strand of dark-brown hair behind her ear, exposing a diamond stud that twinkles in the light from the window.

'I wanted to, but I couldn't get there. I heard from David that your operation went well and you were due to come home any day, so I figured this was easier.'

'But we've known each other for years, Bec. You could've phoned me if you didn't want to come to the hospital, if you couldn't face—'

A cold expression washes across Bec's eyes, enough to make me lean backwards, such is the intensity of her glare.

'What's wrong?'

'I couldn't visit you in your hospital ward or call you. The police were questioning me.'

'Questioning you? Why?'

'Because until earlier this morning, they were convinced I killed Simon.'

I can feel the air leaving my lungs. Black spots dance around at the corner of my vision, and I'm grateful that I'm sitting down. Finally, I blink, the fog clearing a little.

'Why? Why did they think that?'

'How the hell would I know? It must've been something David or Hayley told them when they were questioned, because the first thing I knew about it was when two coppers turned up at the house and insisted I go with them. I've been "helping them with their enquiries" ever since.' She makes quote marks with her fingers, a sardonic twist to her mouth belying the fear in her red-rimmed eyes.

Bloody hell. 'Are you okay?'

'No.'

Chastened, I pick at the skin next to my thumbnail. 'But why would they question you? You were his fiancée.'

'I guess that made me top of that bitch's list of suspects,' she says.

I reach out for the half-full glass of water on the coffee table, and realise my hands are shaking. 'Was that Angela Forbes?'

'Yes.'

The glass lands back on the table with a clatter.

'What have David and Hayley said?' I manage. 'Didn't you speak to them after what happened?'

'I don't know what they've told the police. I just got released, remember? I haven't had a chance to speak with them yet.' She lets out a shaking breath. 'I can't believe this is happening. I can't believe he's dead.'

I swallow, unsure what to say.

Her gaze drops to her lap and she tugs at an

imaginary piece of lint. 'What have the others said to you?'

I snort. 'Next to nothing. Hayley wouldn't tell me anything, and David was elusive as hell. Was Simon ill or something?'

'He never said anything to me. But then he wouldn't, would he?'

'But why would the police think he was murdered? What happened in the escape room, Bec?'

'The lights went out. You panicked – Hayley was calling out to me that you said you'd felt faint and she was really worried about you, and then we tried to bang on the walls to get someone's attention. No one came for ages; by then we realised you were in serious trouble, and Hayley started to scream.'

'I don't remember any of that.'

'David said you were on painkillers.'

'I was, but I didn't think I took that many.'

She raises an eyebrow, the effect ruined by her days-old mascara that has streaked under her lashes. 'You obviously did, otherwise you'd remember, wouldn't you?'

'How long were we stuck in there for?'

'Fifteen minutes. The guy managing the place

must've finally realised something was wrong and opened a side door – God knows what they'd do if there was a fire. Those places are meant to have panic buttons installed. We couldn't even see a fire exit sign.' She shook her head. 'As soon as we saw you, we knew you needed an ambulance – you were delirious, like you had a fever or something. It wasn't until David followed the owner out of the room that we … that we realised Simon hadn't said anything.'

Her lip trembles.

'What happened to him?'

'It looked like he'd tripped trying to find a way out, and hit his head,' she says, and pulls the cuff of her sweater over her hand to wipe at her cheeks. 'David tried CPR, but he didn't respond. They… the ambulance arrived, and I could tell it was bad. They wouldn't let me go with him. The police wouldn't let Hayley or David go either, so they put me in a police car instead and drove me there.'

She takes a gulping breath. 'They said he was dead on arrival.'

I scoot my bum forward so I can reach the coffee table and shove a box of tissues across to her. 'Bec, I'm so sorry.'

She blows her nose, and then chokes out a bitter

laugh. 'Let's not kid ourselves, Lisa. He might have been my ex-fiancé, but he could be an arsehole sometimes.'

Before I can form a response, the front door slams and Bec glances over her shoulder.

'Who's—'

I curse under my breath; we've been so busy talking I haven't heard Barbara's car pull up outside.

'It'll be Mum.'

Bec is already moving, gathering up her bag and hurrying towards the door. 'I didn't realise I'd been here so long. I only meant to pop in for five minutes. I've got to go.'

It's too late.

'Bec – you're still here. Would you like a cup of tea, love?'

Mum is smiling, oblivious to the tension in the room or the guilty look that flits across Bec's face before she shakes her head and forces a smile.

'No, sorry. I have to go.' She forces a smile at me, her lips tight. 'I'll call you, Lisa.'

With that, she's gone.

The front door slams shut in her wake.

'Well, never mind,' says Mum. She recovers

quickly and smooths down her trousers. 'I bought some more orange juice.'

She bustles out the door and within seconds I can hear her in the kitchen, whistling a tune from my eighties childhood.

I let my head drop back against the armchair and let out a groan of frustration.

Why would the police suspect Bec of harming Simon?

17

BEC

THIS END of the tree-lined avenue is English picture-perfect.

Pruned and bare sycamore trees have been diametrically placed at even intervals on the grass verges to avoid entrances to driveways, bright-red post boxes and a cast-iron rubbish bin that bears the local council's logo.

A logo that entailed four management consultancies and upwards of two hundred thousand pounds' worth of ratepayers' taxes.

I know. I paid the invoices.

There are no cars parked on the street. There is no need, not with gravel or concrete driveways that sweep towards four- to five-bedroom houses hidden behind sculpted privet hedgerows.

This isn't the sort of street where you can expect to peer surreptitiously through windows as you pass by.

These people value their privacy.

My two-door hatchback looks all of its eleven years as I approach it, car keys at the ready.

I know I could've parked it outside Lisa's parents' house. I know I could've parked it on their driveway – after all, I always used to.

Used to, but I didn't know if I was going to knock on the door, ring the bell – or run away at the last minute.

I shake off the thought as I cross the road, point the keyring at the car and hear the central locking disengage.

I've parked beyond a newly paved driveway that appears to have had a makeover. Matching terracotta pots adorn the doorstep of the house beyond, the contents of which complement the green hue of the privet hedgerow shielding the front garden from sight.

A man wearing a ridiculous floppy canvas hat suddenly peers around the end of the hedge and glares at me.

'That your car?'

'The blue one?' Christ, I sound scared. I swallow, then try again. 'What about it?'

'It's blocking access for our guests.'

He moves forward, eyebrows knotted together, and it's then that I see the shears in his left hand. He uses them to point towards the road.

'I saw you. You were visiting the Ashtons. Why didn't you park up there?'

'I'm just leaving.'

His top lip curls into a snarl, and then he stomps up the driveway towards the house, calling for someone named Muriel to stop the bloody cat crapping on the flowerbed.

Heat rises to my cheeks, and I glance over my shoulder.

A curtain twitches in the top window of the house opposite, and I turn back to my car.

I fumble the keys as I try to wrench the door open, and for one horrific moment I think they're going to slip from my grasp and drop down the storm drain I've parked across.

They don't, and instead land with a jangled thud onto the carpet lining the footwell.

Exasperated, I toss my bag on the passenger seat, then lean down and reach under the clutch pedal until I can find the keys and shove the right one in the ignition.

I start the car and swerve out into the road as the miserable old git is stalking back towards me.

I slow before I reach Lisa's parents' house.

Her mum's friend's car has gone. She must have dropped Judy off and been on her way before I reached my car. I'd been so absorbed in my own escape that I hadn't noticed she'd left.

My fingers tighten on the steering wheel.

Escape. That's what it was all about. That's what I'd told the police every time they asked. The five of us together again, for the last time.

Escaping the reality of our miserable fucking lives.

I look away from the house, concentrate on the road in front of me, and accelerate past.

Why didn't Lisa know I'd been taken in for questioning?

Hadn't Hayley or David told her?

Did they know?

I reach across to my bag and tug a paper tissue out, braking at the end of the road to let a stream of traffic pass.

I blow my nose and then toss the tissue onto the passenger seat.

The persistent tick-tick of the indicator beats a pattern into my memory. It's like a stopwatch, except it's counting down.

Counting down to the inevitable end.

'Shit.'

A loud blast from the horn on the car behind me sends me skywards out of my seat, rocketing my heartbeat.

I hold up my hand in apology, and accelerate into the gap that's appeared into the traffic, avoiding the glares from the other drivers.

One of them, a woman, shakes her head as I jostle into position, and I bite my lip.

I take a convoluted route back to the two-bedroom end of terrace I rent on the outskirts of town. I don't know what I'm going to do.

The police couldn't find me at home when they first rang the doorbell because I'd been upstairs, throwing up in the bathroom.

Moments later, they'd hammered on the door and when I'd answered, DC Angela Forbes glared at me before introducing herself and then marching me to their car, passing a gloating neighbour by the name of Mrs Dawson.

I was stupid.

I panicked, that's all. When Forbes began to

question me in the interview room at the police station, I froze.

She was patient, going over the details she'd gleaned from my original statement taken at the Accident and Emergency department following Simon's death with an intimacy that was both frustrating and frightening. I was his ex-fiancée, she said, as if that made her more suspicious.

All the time, I tried to second-guess her.

What if I gave a wrong answer? What was the wrong answer? What was the right answer?

If I'd simply focused, given her the basic facts like I'd rehearsed in my mind, it would have been all right. I'd have been in and out of the police station in a matter of minutes. Not the hours I ended up being held.

Exhausted, I park the car two streets away from my house and take a shortcut along an alleyway behind a row of cinderblock garages that have somehow survived since the sixties. I emerge next to a high wooden panelled gate, insert a key into a relatively new padlock and slip back the bolt before peering through the gap.

Not only is my own back garden deserted, but Mrs Dawson is nowhere to be seen either.

I lock the gate, jog to the back door and hurry inside.

There's something going off in the kitchen bin, that much is certain but by the time I empty the refrigerator, take the rubbish outside and then wipe down the worktops, I've convinced myself I'm back in control.

Until I see the photographs lined up along the top shelf above the microwave.

18

LISA

ON THE TELEVISION SCREEN, the forty-something woman wearing a bright-red suit jacket over a white blouse mouths soundlessly, her words replaced with the soft snores emanating from my dad.

He's exhausted; his fishing expedition started at four o'clock this morning and was fruitless, much to Mum's amusement.

While he sleeps, she lets slip that she's sick of cooking brown trout and wishes he'd take up a different hobby in his retirement.

We have quiche instead when he wakes up.

I pick at my food, shaken by Bec's visit and thankful that Mum and Dad don't ask too many questions about my appetite.

I don't want to lie to them, not after everything I've put them through.

We're finishing up when the doorbell rings, silencing our conversation.

'I'll get it,' says Mum, pushing back her chair. She disappears out into the hallway.

I put down my knife and fork, glad that the meal is over and I don't have to pretend anymore. I can't face the food.

Dad wrinkles his nose as I pass my plate to him, gathering up the crockery and cutlery before tipping the scraps into the plastic food bin ready to go out the next morning. He shoves the plates into the dishwasher and is drying his hands on a blue fluffy towel when Mum appears at the doorway with a well-dressed man in his forties who I don't recognise.

He's got black hair peppered with grey that's reflected by his eye colour, his gaze roaming the kitchen until he sets eyes on me at the end of the table.

Mum follows in his wake and clears her throat to get Dad's attention, but the man beats her to the introductions.

'Detective Sergeant Alan Mortlock. I was hoping I could have a few words with Lisa.'

The detective holds out his warrant card to my dad, who takes it from him and inspects it with an air of authority I haven't seen in him since he quit work. He turns the card over in his hands, taking his time before handing it back and folding his arms over his chest. 'She's meant to be recuperating.'

'I realise that, Mr Ashton, but I'm in the middle of an investigation and I need to clarify a few things with your daughter. If we could have a few moments alone?'

Alone?

The nurse's words back at the hospital ring in my ears, about having someone present next time I spoke with the police, and my heart rate skips. I clear my throat, trying to alleviate the dryness that chokes my words.

'What do you want to speak to me about?'

The detective's gaze turns to me. He doesn't smile, but he gestures towards the hallway.

'Do you think we could chat in private? Perhaps the living room?'

I nod. It's evident I don't have a choice.

Dad leads the way, giving a running commentary like an estate agent as he shows the policeman across the hallway and into the living room.

As I follow, I notice there's a second man in the hallway. He's younger than Mortlock, with pale blond hair cut severely close to his scalp. His suit is immaculate.

He doesn't smile, but waits until I shuffle past and then follows me into the room. He stands next to the window, hands crossed in front of his crotch like he's a secret service agent in an action film or something.

Mortlock removes his coat and folds it in his lap as he sits in Dad's armchair before he peers over his shoulder to where Dad is hovering next to the door.

Dad takes the hint.

DS Alan Mortlock wants to talk to me. Alone.

The door to the living room closes behind Dad, and Mortlock turns back to me.

'What do you want?'

He holds up a hand. 'Hang on.'

He goes on to recite a formal caution, the words terrifying me.

'Am I under arrest?'

The younger detective manages a small smile before it disappears, packed away again under a modicum of authority that doesn't quite gel.

'No,' says Mortlock. 'That's the wording we have to use before we speak to you.'

'I've already spoken to the police.'

'I'm aware of that. I apologise for DC Forbes upsetting you. She can be quite enthusiastic about her work.'

'Aggressive and rude, more like. If I've already spoken to DC Forbes, why are you here?'

Mortlock lowers his gaze to his clasped hands. 'Simon's body was released for organ donation immediately by the attending Home Office pathologist who declared him deceased because he'd hit his head. There wasn't any doubt over the cause of death at the time. After reading the initial report, DC Forbes decided to pursue her own enquiries before alerting me.'

So, that's it. Forbes has been poking her nose in without her boss's knowledge.

I pull up the blanket that I discarded earlier, snuggling into it as if I can create a barrier between me and the man in front of me. I'm embarrassed they're here, now, while I'm in yoga pants and an old sweatshirt, vulnerable. 'Why did she arrest Bec?'

'I'm afraid I can't comment about an ongoing investigation,' says Mortlock. 'Have you spoken to your friends? The ones who were in the escape room with you?'

'Yes. Bec was here yesterday. Hayley and David visited me at the hospital.'

'Then you're aware that we're treating Simon Granger's death as suspicious.'

'Why?'

'Again, I can't elaborate. How long had you known him for?'

'Since we were at grammar school together.'

'Was he a boyfriend of yours?'

I wrinkle my nose. I don't like personal questions from strangers, not after all the sessions with the various transplant doctors and surgeons over the past year. I'm tired of being under a microscope.

He's waiting, watching me though. Expecting an answer.

'Only for a while.'

'How long?'

'About a year. Then we split up.'

'When? While you were still at grammar school?'

'Yes. When we were doing our A-levels.'

'You went to the same university as well? By choice?'

'Both of us wanted to study there, and we ended up being offered places at the same time.'

'Interesting.' He glances over at his colleague, who's scratching a ballpoint pen across a black notebook, his brow furrowed in concentration.

The silence spins out, and I realise Mortlock's waiting for me to talk. I read somewhere it's a classic interviewing technique.

I don't give him the satisfaction.

Eventually, he nods as if confident the junior detective has caught up, and then turns his attention back to me.

'Were you aware of any grievances between Simon and your other friends?'

'I wouldn't call them grievances, no. He could be a pain in the arse sometimes.'

That makes him smile. 'In what way?'

I shrug, then wince as the movement pulls my stitches. 'He liked to wind up people. I can't imagine that it'd be serious enough for anyone to want to kill him though.'

'What do you recall? That day you all went to the escape room. It was your birthday, wasn't it?'

I tell him the ragged details I can remember. I blush as I describe taking the painkillers. Having two police officers hanging on my every word makes me feel self-conscious.

When I finish, Mortlock leans back in the armchair, his eyes never leaving mine.

Finally, he gives a slight nod and then stands, gesturing to the other detective who puts away his notebook before turning back to me.

'All right, that's all the questions I have for now. Thank you – we'll see ourselves out.'

When the door to the living room closes, I hear Mum and Dad speaking with Mortlock in the hallway, their voices convivial, helpful.

I sink back into the soft cushions and let out a breath I didn't realise I'd been holding and try to fight down a rising sense of panic that is taking hold.

I need to find out what happened to Simon.

I need to find out if one of my friends is a killer.

19

BEC

I RUB AT HEAVY EYELIDS, and it takes me a moment to wonder why I'm sitting upright.

The room is in darkness.

Thick curtains cover the windows, but through the crack in the material appears a light-grey hue as weak sunlight attempts to break the night's stranglehold.

A solitary blackbird sings beyond the glass, a multi-note chirp that used to fill me with joy.

Now it reminds me that I have to face another day.

I've got my bearings now. Since moving in, I've added cheap or second-hand furniture to the meagre belongings I'd brought from Simon's place when we'd split up.

I fell asleep in the overstuffed armchair I bought in a charity shop, and now I stare at the threads I picked from the arms last night and wonder if it'd be simpler to throw it away.

I wince as I uncurl my legs, cramp seizing my calf muscles.

My toe catches the wineglass, the soft chink of cheap crystal on exposed floorboards reaching me a split second before I remember I didn't finish the Pinot Noir.

I groan as I lean forward and contemplate the puddle of red that pools next to my feet, and then gasp as I realise it will reach the discarded photographs unless I move.

Galvanised into action, I sweep the photos from the floor and lob them onto a low table already piled high with magazines before hauling myself upright and heading to the kitchen.

Moments later, I return with paper kitchen towel and a tea towel soaked in water and wipe up the spilt wine, grateful at least that the glass didn't shatter but wrinkling my nose at the smell.

I pad out to the kitchen, throw away the sodden paper towel and chuck the cloth in the washing machine, before I switch on the kettle.

I change my mind as it starts to boil and pour a

pint of water from the filter jug instead, finishing half in four deep gulps. I drink the rest, and stand, panting, staring at the mobile phone next to the microwave.

It's dead, despite being plugged in. In my stupor last night, I'd forgotten to flick the switch on the socket.

I didn't mean to drink so much. I couldn't sleep.

I tried, but the nightmares woke me up. When I checked my watch, it was only one o'clock in the morning, but I knew it was pointless lying there in the dark, so I got up and came downstairs.

The phone is flat because I played games on it for two hours straight while I worked my way through the first half of the red. I didn't go on social media – I haven't used it in years, so I've never put the apps on my phone. I stared at the screen and played game after game of Solitaire and then when I grew bored with that, switched to Sudoku.

None of it worked.

The photographs taunted me, teased me, beckoned until I slid the phone aside and picked up the first of the three silver frames.

We'd swapped places by the time this photograph was taken. I was wearing Hayley's reindeer antlers and she was the one behind the camera.

Greg was holding up his fingers behind Lisa's head and laughing – she'd moaned about not having any antlers of her own to wear, and he'd obliged.

I run my thumb over his face.

Behind him, David's expression is hard to read. He's glancing sideways at Lisa, his mouth tight. I didn't realise he wasn't smiling at the time.

Trust Hayley to take a photograph when someone wasn't ready for the camera.

Four of us were eighteen in this image; David had had his birthday a couple of months before, then Lisa in November.

Already, a rivalry had begun between the three boys as each of them jostled for position within our group. Simon always won.

It helped, I think, that Simon and Lisa split up months before starting university.

I didn't know any of them before then. Although five of us lived in the same city, we grew up in different suburbs, or – in David's case – one of the outlying villages, and apart from Simon and Lisa, attended different schools.

Hayley and I ended up sharing a house with

two others near the campus, Simon and Lisa both stayed at their respective parents' houses in order to save money, which left Greg and David in the halls of residence.

It makes Simon's death harder to bear.

We're local, and people will talk.

I push the photograph aside and pick up another – our graduation day, five years ago.

God, we look happy.

Five years, and yet it could have been a lifetime ago.

I remember the exhilaration being tinged with a sense of dread. Since I was five years old, I'd been part of the academic system. Seventeen years of study and organised structure.

The future was terrifying.

Suddenly it didn't matter what your grades were, what the best TV show was, which celebrity we'd like to shag.

It was all about employment prospects (dismal), careers, future mortgages – being an adult.

Greg isn't in the photograph.

We hadn't seen him for over two years by then.

No one had.

No one talked about it. That's what we'd agreed.

Simon and I got together properly two years ago. We hadn't seen each other for a while, and it had been Lisa who'd suggested we all catch up "for old times' sake". We'd arrived at the restaurant near the marina before anyone else.

He'd bought me a drink and we had wandered out to the deck to watch the sailing boats come in before sunset, the air around us full of conversation and laughter as people eased into the weekend.

Lisa was delighted when she found out Simon and I had spent the rest of that weekend together, claiming full responsibility with a knowing smile. It made it all the more unforgivable when I discovered for myself what she hadn't told me about him.

What he was really like.

I don't know if we're ever going to get past that now.

I drop the photograph to the table and scramble from the armchair, then pull back the curtains to reveal a mediocre morning sky, all grey clouds and drizzle.

The living room is musty, cloying, and I need a bath.

I find my tablet computer in the bedroom, find a music playlist I love in the hope it will silence the thoughts going around in my head, and cross to the bathroom.

As I run a generous portion of bath soak into the churning water, I stagger. I'm still exhausted, too tired, too anxious.

Steam rises from the surface of the water as I lean over and twist the taps, the cold one refusing to close properly so that a steady *drip-drip* beats a rhythm that echoes off the tiles.

I can't stop it – the memory of Greg's face that night resurfaces, and I shiver.

Why the hell did David think an escape room was a good way to celebrate Lisa's birthday, when we can't even escape our past?

20

HAYLEY

THE CAFÉ IS LOCATED on the corner of two busy streets.

Outside, there are six wrought-iron tables that are fought over as much as last-minute deals in a Black Friday sale. Red and white striped shade cloths dangle from the windows, offering shelter from drizzle or sunlight but not much else.

It's too cold to sit outside today. An icy wind whips at the shade cloths as if it's trying to rip them away. Grey-black clouds are forming over the tops of tower blocks in the distance, threatening heavy rain.

I smile my thanks at the good-looking man who holds the door open for me, but falter when he leaves without a second glance. Blushing, I turn my attention to the pastries and sandwiches that lie amongst fake greenery in the counter beside me.

An Italianate decor fills the inside of the café; black and white photographs from films by Pasolini and Fellini adorn dark wooden panelled walls alongside 1950s advertisements for olive oil and landscape photographs of the Tuscan countryside. Sinatra croons along in the background with Dean and Sammy.

The bitter aroma of coffee fills the air, which is filled with the clatter of plates, glasses, china cups and a steady roar as the café fills for the lunchtime rush.

It's a place to be seen and to be revered, and I have no idea why I've come here. Except that it's familiar, and I need that right now.

I need to feel like I belong.

I need to feel like everything is normal, as it was.

As it will never be again.

I'm tucked away in a corner at a square wooden table with a red and white chequered cloth laid over it, set for two people. I shove the cutlery aside as the waitress wanders over, order a pot of green tea, then pull my iPad from my handbag and sit with my back to the wall.

The light from the front windows can't reach me here. Above my head is a metal lantern, a candle-shaped low wattage bulb providing enough light that my eyes won't suffer from screen glare while still allowing me to sit unnoticed by anyone entering the café.

I crane my neck to read the free Wi-Fi code the café's owner has helpfully scrawled on a blackboard sign next to the counter, and log in to my emails.

Running my own business has been a revelation. When I first took the plunge, I'd been made redundant and had no idea where I was going to find work. Cleaning other people's houses became a necessity rather than a career calling, but then the word-of-mouth recommendations kept coming in, and a year ago I had so much work on that I could employ six part-time staff and retired from having to stick brushes down strangers' toilets.

Now I manage the back office – bookings and payroll – and let my capable team of five women and one man tidy up after our clients' mess.

I glance up as the waitress places a white china pot and matching cup and saucer on the table, thank her with a smile and then close my emails and open a web browser.

The screen defaults to a search engine and my fingers hover over the keypad.

Do I want to know?

Yes.

I type in two words, Simon Granger, and then hit the 'Enter' key.

It takes all of two seconds for the results to appear, starting with three Facebook profiles and five from LinkedIn. I scroll past those until I see the first of the news stories.

Local man's death in escape room treated as suspicious.

There it is, then. It's official.

There's nothing I can do about it now.

It's too late.

I keep my chin down but raise my gaze to the room, sweeping my eyes across the other people sitting at tables, queueing at the counter, serving the customers.

Do they know what I've done?

As a business owner, I guard my reputation with pride. I'm dependable, trustworthy, loyal. I make sure my employees meet the necessary prerequisites for police checks and everything. I project the aura of a top-end business for middle class customers.

My business is the luxury you haven't realised you need. When I visit my clients' homes to assess their needs, that's what I tell them. That's what's printed on the postcards I pay thousands to be distributed amongst the most affluent addresses in the area, to the ones who I know can afford it.

My eyes fall back to the iPad, and I frown.

There's an opinion piece. A reporter by the name of Stella Barrett has put in her two cents' worth about the death of Simon Granger. Lisa Ashton is mentioned. The oh-my-god-what-are-the-chances story about her last-minute kidney transplant are set out across what would be a double-page spread in a print edition.

I wonder if Lisa or her family have seen it.

Despite myself, despite my fear, I smile. It's about time she took some of the blame. Some of the flack. Some of the guilt.

And then I read on, and see that Bec has been named as well.

My heart lurches. No, no, no. That wasn't meant to happen.

I find her number in my phone, but there's no answer. It says the phone is switched off, so there's no option to leave a voicemail message.

I push back my chair, run to the back of the café and push open the door to the ladies' toilet, reaching the stall just in time.

I PEEL AWAY a corner of the dressing that covers a square of my abdomen, and immediately regret my decision.

A rushing sound fills my ears as my eyes take in the scar that punctures my right side. I couldn't look when the community nurse came around to change it yesterday, nor when I had my post-operation check-up at the hospital before that.

A series of neat stitches are prominent within my bruised skin, and I groan.

'Lisa? You all right in there?' The handle lowers a second after Dad's voice calls out, but the bathroom door is locked.

'I'm fine,' I manage, and press the bandage back into place.

A corner sticks up, refusing to stay in place and I curse under my breath.

'Best unlock the door, love. In case you have a fall. The doctor said you could be light-headed for a few days yet.'

I stand up and shuffle towards the bathroom cabinet. 'Okay.'

The floorboard outside the door creaks as Dad moves away, but I'm not interested – I rifle through the contents of the middle drawer, sure I've seen a box of plasters tucked away near the back. Mind you, that was several months ago. I was still wearing heels for a start, which explained why I needed the plasters back then.

My fingers touch cardboard and I give a small cheer under my breath, then remove two plasters from the box to tape down the end of the bandage before straightening to admire my handiwork.

I take a step back in shock at the grey pallor of my face in the mirror, and stumble backwards.

'Shit.'

Everything exploded half an hour ago.

Mum and Dad don't usually buy a Sunday paper. They get the Saturday one with the TV listings in it, and that's it. As long as they know what's on catch-up and streaming, all is right with the world. Everything else can go to hell in a bucket.

Which is what it's just done, because Mum decided she wanted to read the winter gardening special in the local rag's Sunday supplement.

They're putting a brave face on it, of course.

I'm not.

Somehow, a journalist found out that Bec was taken in for questioning. That Simon's ex-fiancée is a suspect in his untimely death. That when he died, another of his ex-girlfriends – me – got one of his kidneys.

It's splashed across the front page in black, bold letters – *Man Murdered to Save Ex-Girlfriend*.

Underneath that, a subtitle: *Local man's death in escape room treated as suspicious.*

Dad took the landline off the hook after the first phone call, and both of them have switched off their mobile phones.

That first call was from another newspaper, the journalist telling Dad that if he didn't provide them with a quote, they'd make something up. And they will.

The paper that printed the story this morning didn't ask any of us to comment – it's pure conjecture and speculation, but the damage is done.

I flip down the wooden toilet seat, then sink onto it and start to scroll through social media again. My account has always been locked to private, but I can clearly see the comments targeting me and my friends in my news feed. There's even a hashtag trending.

I nearly drop the phone as it rings, and David's name appears on the screen.

'Hang on,' I say when I answer, then unlock the bathroom door and pad along to the bedroom. 'Okay, I can talk now.'

'I'm so sorry, Lisa,' he says. 'I've just seen the paper. Have the police been in touch about it?'

'No. Not yet, anyway. Do you think they will?'

'I'm sure they'll have something to say about it,' he says. 'I mean, the press can't go around saying stuff like that, can they?'

I manage a small smile at his innocence. 'They do it all the time. It sells newsprint. Well, and advertising space. That's all we are to them. Have you managed to speak to Bec? I tried to phone her earlier but it keeps going through to voicemail.'

'Same. I was going to drive around to hers to check on her. I wondered if you'd spoken to her today.'

I sink onto the edge of the bed and run my

hand over the cotton duvet. 'I can't imagine what she's going through. I'm worried about her, David. She seemed distant when she was around here yesterday.'

'In what way?'

'Reluctant to talk much. I mean, I know she's grieving but when Mum turned up, she bolted. I've never seen her like that before.'

'That's not good.' He pauses a moment, and then— 'Have you remembered anything else about that day at the escape room?'

'No. I keep going over it in my mind, but once I get to the part where Hayley was helping me along, I get stuck. I can't remember what happened next.'

I can hear my voice getting higher, my heart rate increasing.

'Try not to worry,' David says. 'You've got to concentrate on getting better. I'll pop around to Bec's to make sure she's okay.'

'Thank you.'

I push myself to my feet, wincing as the dressing pulls against my stitches, then wander across to the window.

The house backs onto another housing estate, leylandii trees creating a screen between the properties. Mum has planted shrubs down the earth borders that frame the lawn that is Dad's pride and joy, wooden fences separating it from the next-door properties.

Mum and Dad's neighbour is painting the side of his shed, and raises a hand when he spots me at the window.

'Are you still there?'

David's voice cuts through my meandering thoughts, and I turn away from the glass.

'I'm still here. Just thinking.' I exhale, letting some of the stress leave my body. 'You should go. Go and check on Bec. Let me know?'

'I will.' His voice changes, ready to end the call, then as if having second thoughts, he's back. 'And, Lisa? Stay away from the TV for a while. I have a feeling this is going to get worse before it gets better.'

22

DAVID

WHAT ELSE DO THEY KNOW?

I've never heard of the journalist who was named on the byline. After I finish scrolling through the story again on my phone, I have to run to the bathroom, losing my meagre breakfast down the bowl and rinsing out my mouth with water straight from the tap.

A thin line of sweat bubbles at my temples, and I wipe it away with the back of my hand.

I brush my teeth, then hurry back to the bedroom and pull on a sweatshirt before taking the stairs two at a time, wrenching open the front door.

My hand shakes as I raise the key fob to the car and press the button to unlock it. I switch off the radio as soon as it blares from the speakers. I don't want to hear pop songs, and I don't want to listen to mindless chit-chat while I'm driving over to Bec's place.

I don't want to hear the news.

Somehow, neither my nor Hayley's names have been mentioned in the article. The bloke who owns the escape room refused to comment, according to the journalist – probably on the advice of his solicitor, I assume – and there's no word that the police are going to say anything about the story yet.

I wonder what I would do if I were in Bec's shoes.

I'd be angry. Scared. Lost.

I wouldn't know who I'd ask for help. None of us has any legal experience. None of us has ever had to deal with the press before, let alone be subjected to accusations like those made this morning.

I blink as a car horn blasts, and pull back into the left lane, my heart lurching.

The taxi driver holds up his middle finger as he passes, his brow furrowed as he mouths the accompanying insult.

I need to concentrate. I need to get to Bec's house and make sure she's okay.

We live five miles from each other, and I've only

driven there once. I prefer to cycle. Driving makes me anxious. I didn't learn to drive until I left university, and I don't get enough practice in to be confident at it.

I should've bought an automatic, too. As I slow for a T-junction up ahead, I grind the gears into second. Heat rises in my cheeks as a woman pushing a pram along the pavement next to me stops to stare, and I brake awkwardly.

A cyclist swerves to avoid the bonnet of the car as he shoots past.

I eye the back of the carbon frame with envy as he recedes into the distance, then turn my attention back to the road.

I go right, and see the sign for the leisure centre ahead. Bec's house is about half a mile past it, and I can't recall whether there's parking outside.

I don't know where to leave the car if I can't park outside. I don't know this part of town that well. Apart from visiting Bec, I never need to be here.

I eye my mobile phone in the cup holder between the front seats. I never use the dashboard clip for it that came with the car; I can't concentrate if I'm having a phone conversation at the same time, and would get distracted every time a message alert popped up on the screen.

I should've pulled over a mile or so ago and tried to call Bec again, but it's too late now.

I'm nearly there.

I breathe a sigh of relief as I approach her house, slowing down, and see a car space at the kerb. After a panicked effort at parallel parking, I manage it without causing damage to mine or the other vehicles and climb out.

The curtains are pulled but I can't see anything from here on the pavement. I push open the wooden gate and dial her number once more as I negotiate the cracked concrete path. A curtain twitches in the front window of the house to the left, and I glare. The curtain falls back into place. There's no answer on the phone and I shove it into the back pocket of my jeans before rapping my knuckles on the front door and ringing the bell.

When Bec doesn't appear, I bend down and flip open the plastic letterbox flap.

'Bec? It's David. Are you in there?'

I peer through, twisting my head to get a better angle.

The door to the living room is open, but there is no sound and the kitchen seems quiet, too.

'Bec?'

Nothing.

I straighten, then turn and rest my hands on my hips, unsure what to do.

The street is quiet, the morning commuter rush over hours ago. I'm surprised there are no journalists hanging about; no one watching the house in the hope of an exclusive comment from Bec.

I'm relieved, too.

I take a couple of steps back and raise my eyes to the bedroom window above the front door. Bec's house is tiny – main bedroom at the front, a smaller one and a tiny bathroom at the back.

She'd have heard me. She must have done.

If she was okay.

It's no good. I'm panicking now. I need to find her.

I hurry back to the road, ignore the way the car is parked four inches away from the kerb with the bonnet sticking out, risking a clipped mirror at least, and turn left.

There's an alleyway three doors along that I recall from a drunken night returning to Bec's when she didn't want to piss off her neighbours. It runs along the back of the terraced properties, a narrow pathway that stinks of dog shit and rotten undergrowth. I peer over the fence, counting the houses until I'm sure I'm at the back of Bec's and then swear under my breath.

She's fitted a new padlock to the gate, and I don't have a key.

I can't see anything through the windows at the back of the house, and, reasoning that she won't answer the phone if I try to call again, I check to make sure none of the neighbours are watching.

Satisfied I won't be seen, I clamber over the fence and hurry to the back door.

It's locked.

The mottled patio stones outside the back door are offset by colourful pots that Bec has planted with herbs and flowers, and I start lifting each of them, trying to remember which one she'd hidden the spare key under that last time we got locked out, and hoping she hasn't changed that lock as well. Eventually I find it under a large oregano plant, the smell reminding me of pizzas, and hurry back to the door.

The key turns easily, and I step over the threshold.

'Bec?' I call her, softly, and then once more. 'Bec? Are you there?'

There's still no answer.

I have to find her.

I'M at home in the office I created from the dining room space, a dappled light stretching through the patio windows and playing on the beech surface of the table where I've spread all the paperwork in an attempt to make some sense of it all.

I'm humming under my breath; I don't recognise the tune and I'm not trying too hard to fathom where it comes from. I only want to forget.

A clutch of lilies fills the crystal vase on the corner of the table, the bright-yellow petals lending a cheerfulness to the space that doesn't quite fit my mood.

I've tried to phone Bec two more times since coming home. I wonder if I should go around to her house, to see if she's all right, and bite my lip. I probably should've done that as soon as I left the café but I felt so sick, it was all I could do to drive home.

My mobile phone vibrates, and I'm torn from the contract I've been trying to read.

I jump in my seat, the noise jerking me from my thoughts.

It's David.

I lower the stapled pages to the desk and spin the chair around as I pick up the phone.

'What's up?'

'It's Bec, you've got to come over.'

He sounds out of breath, panicked even. Not like the David I know.

'You're at her house?'

'She wouldn't answer her phone. Lisa couldn't get hold of her, either so I drove over.'

'You drove?'

It must be serious if David used his car. He hates driving.

There's a pause, then: 'Yes.'

'What's going on?'

'I've called an ambulance—'

'What? Why—'

'She's tried to kill herself, Hayley. That fucking reporter.'

He starts stumbling over his words, and I can't understand what he's trying to tell me.

'Stay there. I'm coming.'

I'm already moving, tugging on my shoes as I end the call before swiping my car keys and handbag from the bottom of the stairs.

I burst through the front door, tear along the pavement to where my car's parked at the end of the street, and stomp on the accelerator as soon as the key's turned.

Not Bec. Please, not Bec.

We only live thirty or forty minutes apart, but if feels like an age before I get there.

I should have come sooner. I should have been here for her.

I see blue flashing lights halfway down her street as I turn the corner, the wheels clipping the kerb in my haste to reach her.

Fighting down bile, my stomach muscles clenching painfully, I slow as I approach her house. There's a fleeting moment, a vain hope that I'm wrong, and then reality punches me in the solar plexus, leaving me breathless.

The ambulance is outside Bec's, and there's a police car parked behind it.

I slam on the brakes, snatch up my handbag

and leap from the car without locking it, my focus wholly on the crowd gathered at the side of the ambulance.

I don't recognise anyone.

I can't see David.

As I reach the ambulance, I realise there's someone inside it. One of the crew peers out from the open door, and as he moves to the side, I see a slight figure with a shock of brown hair on the stretcher inside.

'Bec?'

'You can't see her.' The ambulance officer holds up his hand and steps sideways to block my view so I can't see her now.

'Please, you have to tell me where you're taking her. I'm a friend.'

The man's features soften, and he leans towards me, his eyes raking the faces behind us. 'The local casualty unit,' he says. 'We've just heard they've got room for her so we don't have to try to get her over to the city hospital.'

He watches me for a moment, as if trying to transmit another message, and then I get it.

'She won't make it if she has to travel any further, will she?'

'She's lost a lot of blood. We have to go. I'm sorry.'

I nod, then step back as he leaps into the back of the ambulance and closes the door in my face.

The sirens begin to wail and then they're off, disappearing in a blur of blue and panic.

My ears are still ringing and I don't notice the presence beside me until a mobile phone is thrust under my nose and a woman wearing too much make-up gives me a predatory smile.

'Do you know Rebecca Wallis?'

'Pardon?'

'The ex-girlfriend. The one who killed Simon Granger. Did you know her? What do you think she's feeling right now? Has she tried to take her life before?'

I blink. I can't think straight. Who is this woman? How does she know Bec?

'Who are you?'

'Stella Barrett, *Daily News*.'

Shit, she's the journalist who wrote the story about Bec.

'You bitch.'

There's a blur to my left and then David lunges at the reporter, spittle flying from his mouth.

I haven't seen him this angry before. His face is

flushed red, his eyes wide as he elbows past an elderly man to reach her, his hands outstretched as if to throttle her.

He doesn't make it.

A female police officer pushes away from the side of the patrol car. She might be several inches shorter than David, but she grabs his sleeve and uses his momentum to spin him around.

His body collides with the side of the car and there's a collective gasp from the onlookers as he staggers, his knees buckling.

'Come on.' The police officer steadies him and then raises a hand towards the reporter. 'Back off. Now.'

The journalist is wearing a smug expression before turning away; it doesn't matter what anyone else says now as she scurries along the pavement.

Moments later, a bright-red sports car screeches away, and I resign myself to the knowledge that she got what she wanted.

A victim, and another story.

I turn back to David. The police officer has her hand on his shoulder, speaking to him in a low voice. I can't make out whether she's cautioning him about going after the journalist or apologising for the way she swung him into the side of the car, but David's face is grim.

His mouth is set into a thin line, his brow furrowed. He stares at the house as the police officer talks to him, refusing to meet the woman's eyes.

After a while, she pats David on the arm and walks over to her colleague. Her expression is petulant; she overreacted, and she knows it.

Some of Bec's neighbours are walking away shaking their heads, muttering under their breath about what has transpired right outside their front doors. The old man who David pushed past glares at him, then turns on his heel and crosses the road. He doesn't look back.

I try to focus.

'David, we need to go. We need to get to the hospital.'

He's still glaring at the house, his expression blank.

'David?'

He shakes his head as if to try and break the spell, then stares at me. 'What?'

I take hold of his arm and begin to pull him towards my car as I explain. 'Hospital. Now. They've taken Bec—'

My phone begins a shrill interruption. I glance

down at the screen, and bite back the groan that threatens to escape.

It's Lisa.

I glance across at David who is walking along the pavement as if in a trance and I wonder if this is it.

If this is when it all unravels.

I'm PACING the bedroom that was once mine, then wasn't, and now is.

It was requisitioned in my absence since those university days; the dreamcatcher that hung in the window is now in a box, one of many stacked in a corner of the garage, and Dad had the wallpaper replaced before I moved back in after selling my flat last year.

I stare blankly at the fine details in the embossed print, my mind racing.

It's now two hours since David phoned, and he hasn't called back. Nor is he answering the eight calls I've tried to make to him. Each and every one has gone through to voicemail.

I stopped leaving messages after the second one, aware of the rising panic in my voice and scaring myself.

I keep checking the screen though, willing him to get in touch.

I've tried Bec's number, but the same thing happens. No answer, and it goes to voicemail after three rings.

Hayley is ignoring me, too – I've called her twice; the first time it went to voicemail, the second time it cut out as if someone had hit the reject button.

I don't know what to do.

'Lisa?'

I stop pacing as the door opens and Mum peers around it.

'You okay?' Her lips thin into a tight smile. 'You'll wear out the carpet.'

I say nothing.

'What's going on, love?'

She moves to the single bed, smooths the flower-patterned duvet, and then sits. She pats the space next to her.

'Come and sit down.'

I sigh. I haven't got a choice, not when I'm a guest in Mum and Dad's home now.

She reaches out and tucks a stray strand of hair behind my ear as I join her, exactly like she's done for as long as I can remember. The gesture brings tears to my eyes and I wipe at them with the back of my sleeve.

I choke out a laugh. I've regressed to my fourteen-year-old self, bawling over the unfairness of life.

'Come on,' she says. 'Talk to me. What's going on?'

'We can't get hold of Bec.'

'What do you mean?'

I hold up my useless phone. 'She's not answering. David tried to call her earlier as well, and she didn't answer then either. He went around there to make sure she was okay after that— after the—'

'Oh, Lisa.'

Mum wraps her arm around me as the tears flow.

I've never felt so pathetic in my life.

'I haven't heard anything, Mum. He's not answering his phone, either.'

'They're probably talking. Probably haven't heard the phones if they're in a different room.'

I take the paper tissue she holds out to me and

blow my nose, then straighten my shoulders. 'Maybe. I think I should go around there.'

'How?' Mum's voice is startled. 'You can't go anywhere. You need to rest.'

'I start physio next week, Mum, and I'm having loads of check-ups at the hospital. I can't sit around forever, and I need to know that Bec's okay.'

'Still, that doesn't mean you can go rushing off. What happens if—'

We both jump as the phone next to me vibrates. There's a cheerful *ping* and a text appears as I pick it up.

'It's David.'

'What does it say?'

I scan the words, bile rising in my throat. 'It's Bec. They've taken her to hospital. She tried to kill herself.'

Mum gasps, her hand to her mouth. 'Bec? Will she be okay?'

'I don't know. Hang on.'

I quickly type a reply, and pace the carpet while I wait for David's response. I nearly drop the phone when it vibrates again, then I squint at the screen.

'He says he found her. There was blood everywhere. She slit her wrists. The ambulance just left.'

Mum's standing next to me now, coaxing me, steering me back to the bed. I sink onto it, leaning against her as I try to absorb the news.

'What else does he say? Is she going to be all right?'

'Nothing.'

'Give him a call.'

She gives me an encouraging nudge, and I don't hesitate.

I frown after three attempts. 'He's still not answering. He can't be driving – he wouldn't have sent the texts.'

'Perhaps Hayley is with him?'

'Maybe.'

The fourth call goes through to voicemail again and I drop the phone into my lap. 'I need to go to the hospital.'

Mum's shaking her head, her eyes wide. 'It's better that you stay here. David will send another text when he knows what's going on.'

'I'm not sitting around doing nothing while I wait to hear from him. I need to be there for Bec. I wasn't there for her when the police came around to question her. I need to be there now.'

I stand before she can try to stop me, and turn

back to face her as I realise I'm still not allowed to drive.

'I don't suppose you could give me a lift, could you?'

25

DAVID

I REST my elbows on my knees and stare at the tiled floor, then swallow.

My throat is dry and every time I inhale the sickness worsens.

Hayley has stopped asking me if I'm okay.

She freaked out earlier when she realised my hands were covered in blood. She wouldn't let me touch anything in her car, and guided me out of it after releasing the seatbelt, a look of horror and disgust clouding her face. As soon as we reached the Accident and Emergency ward, she pointed to the sign for the public toilets.

I scrubbed hard at my skin, turning it from red to pink as the blood washed away while all the time I wondered where Bec was.

Where they had taken her.

'Here.'

I raise my eyes to find a coffee cup dangling in front of me.

'Thanks.'

I take it from Hayley and she drops into the hard plastic seat next to mine, crossing her legs before taking a sip of her own drink, watching the hospital staff bustle back and forth.

Her expression is hard to read but it seems she's looking down her nose at them, as if running her own business puts her head and shoulders above everyone else.

Me, I'm in awe of the people who work here.

They wear different coloured shirts – I suppose dependent upon their expertise – and move with a determination that leaves the rest of us in their wake.

None of them will talk to us, though. Bec's parents are on the way, and we're not family.

Not important enough.

'What made you go there?' Hayley says.

I sit upright; the sound of her voice after so many moments' silence is a welcome relief and I seize upon it. 'Neither me or Lisa could get hold of her on the phone. You know what Bec's normally like. She can never ignore a call. She has to answer it.'

'This week has been anything but normal. Maybe after everything that's happened to her, she didn't want to talk.'

'Obviously.'

We fall silent once more, the conversations around us becoming a white noise to the silence that drags out between us.

It's strange, me and Hayley being here.

Out of the five of us, we were never the closest. We're fine within the group, with Lisa and Bec – and Simon, once – to absorb us. Here, just us, it feels strained.

'What happened?'

Hayley's voice is little more than a whisper, but I understand why.

There's a middle-aged man sitting in a chair on the opposite side of the corridor to us, and he hasn't stopped sneaking glances our way since we sat down. I'm sure he recognises us, even though neither of our photographs appeared in the newspaper report. Maybe he was outside Bec's house, one of those trying to crane their necks to find out what was going on.

I don't trust him, and it seems Hayley has the same thought.

I lean closer to her, keeping my voice low.

'I couldn't get any answer on the phone or by banging on the front door. When I looked through the letterbox, I could see her handbag so I figured she hadn't gone out. The curtains upstairs were closed. I tried calling through the letterbox but I couldn't hear her, so I went around the back. I knew where she kept the back door key.'

Hayley turns in her chair and raises an eyebrow.

I hold up my hand before she can say anything. 'I went home with her once; we were drunk – we got to the front door before she realised she'd lost her keys. She keeps the spare one for the back door under a plant pot. The oregano, if you must know.'

I see her shoulders relax a little and she gestures for me to continue.

'She'd been cleaning; I could smell the lemon scented stuff she uses. Downstairs was tidy, but there was no sign of her.'

'Why did you go upstairs? She could've been out somewhere.'

'Really? When was the last time you knew Bec to go out and not take her phone with her?'

'Where was it?'

'Plugged in on the kitchen worktop, switched off.' I shrug, avoiding the man's intense stare.

He folds his hands in his lap and turns his gaze towards the nurses' station, finding something interesting there to stare at instead of us, for a change.

'I don't know,' I say. 'I had this feeling that something was wrong, what with her phone left there and her bag in the hallway. She wasn't in the living room so I went upstairs, checked her bedroom, and then opened the bathroom door.'

Hayley reaches out for my hand, and squeezes.

I close my eyes. It's the closest we've been in a long time.

'I think I knew before I opened the door what I'd see, but I never thought there would be so much—'

'It's okay,' says Hayley. 'You found her, David. She's here, because of you.'

'She looked so peaceful. She'd even some music on. Remember that song we always used to try to dance to on New Year's Eve at uni?'

Hayley manages a smile. She squeezes my hand once more and then releases it as a couple in their late sixties approach the nurses' station at the end of the corridor and speak in hushed tones.

'That's them,' she says. 'That's Bec's mum and dad, isn't it?'

They haven't aged well.

I recall photographs I'd seen of a spritely couple who spent the summers sailing in the Mediterranean and the winters skiing in Bulgaria. Or maybe that's why their faces seem so lined and creased now; all that ultra-violet sun damage.

The nurse speaks to them, and then points in our direction.

Bec's dad glances over his shoulder, noticing us for the first time. His shoulders slump, and then they're moving towards us.

I notice the man opposite us straighten in his seat, and I pull Hayley to her feet and glare at him.

'Come on,' I say pointedly. 'Let's find somewhere more private to talk.'

We meet Bec's parents at the end of the corridor and I shake their hands. Hayley is pulled into a hug by Bec's mother; the gesture instinctive in the midst of this latest tragedy.

'Any news?' Bec's dad's voice is gruff, his eyes red.

I shake my head. 'They won't tell us; we're not family. Will they let you in to see her?'

'Yes. They've managed to do a successful blood

transfusion and treat her wounds but the nurse doesn't think she'll be conscious for a few hours.' Bec's mum dabs at her eyes with a paper tissue. 'I can't believe this is happening.'

Nor can I.

'We were told you were the one who found her,' says Bec's dad. 'You phoned the ambulance?'

'Straight away,' I tell him. 'I didn't know what else to do.'

He takes me by the hand again, but this time he doesn't let go.

'You saved my Bec,' he says. 'You saved our daughter.'

26

HAYLEY

I STIFLE a yawn and peer at the clock on the wall at the end of the corridor, then swear under my breath.

It feels like we've been waiting here for ages and, as well as having a numb arse from sitting on the plastic chair, I'm bored.

I don't understand why anyone would want to work somewhere like this. The pay is supposed to be atrocious, it's obvious the hours are hell, and from the harassed expressions the two women on the nurses' desk are wearing as they stab their fingers at computer keyboards and telephones, they're understaffed as well.

And that smell.

Cloying. Chemical-drenched. Clinical.

It was bad enough having to come here to visit Lisa last week, but this? This is worse.

Why didn't Bec tell any of us she'd been taken in for questioning by the police? We've known each other for over seven years; surely that counts for something.

What the hell did she tell them?

I ignore the thought that creeps up unawares, battening it down.

Now is not the time.

I clear my throat and am about to ask David to buy us another coffee when the double doors at the entrance into the Accident and Emergency wing slide open, and Lisa arrives with her mum in tow.

I can't help the gasp that escapes my lips.

She is pale.

Too pale.

The effort it must've taken to haul herself into her mum's car and then walk from the car park outside to here has been too much for her.

Instantly, I'm on my feet, hurrying towards her.

'Lisa? You should've waited at home.'

The stricken expression on her face says it all. 'I had to come. Is there any news?'

'Not yet. The doctors won't tell us anything

because we're not family, but Bec's parents turned up—'

'Where is she? Is she okay?'

I place my hands on her arms and give her a gentle hug. 'She's going to be all right. David found her in time.'

She sags against me, and I hold her for a moment.

'You shouldn't hang around.' David's voice cuts through my thoughts and I release her, stepping to one side.

He's standing next to Judy, glowering. 'You need to go home.'

'But I want to see her.' Lisa's voice is irritable, defensive. 'After everything she's been through, she needs all of us here to support her. It's the least we can do.'

'None of us can see her at the moment. It's family only.' He takes a step towards her. 'Go home. If you catch something here – even a cold or something – it could set back your recovery.'

'That's what I said.' Judy sighs, and places a hand on her daughter's arm. 'Come on. Before you catch a chill.'

Lisa turns to me, her eyes pleading. 'I can stay, can't I?'

'I promise I'll phone you the moment we have any news,' I say. 'We're probably going to head off in a moment anyway. I don't think they'll be letting any visitors in to see Bec for at least another twenty-four hours. I'd imagine in cases like this they'll want to do all sorts of assessments, right?'

I turn to David for support, and he nods.

'Absolutely.' He jerks his thumb over his shoulder. 'I don't think they're going to tell us much today. Go home, Lisa. Go and rest.'

Her shoulders relax a little, and she nods, her gaze to the floor. 'I suppose you're right. I just panicked when I heard. After everything else—'

'Excuse me? Lisa Ashton?'

I swivel on my heel and come face to face with the man who was sitting opposite me and David. Now he's thrusting a smartphone at Lisa, a hungry look in his eyes.

'Who are you?' she says. She takes a step back. 'What do you want?'

'Scott Nash, *Daily Post*. How do you feel about the woman who killed Simon Granger trying to take her own life after saving yours?'

'What?'

Judy has a hand to her mouth, the other reaching out to her daughter, hauling her away from the journalist who is side-stepping around her to try to get the soundbite he so desperately needs.

Before I can stop him, David has his hand on the man's coat collar, dragging him away, a snarl on his lips. What he lacks in brawn, David makes up for in height and he wastes no time in frog-marching Nash away from Lisa.

The journalist shrugs off his grip, then smiles at Lisa. 'We'll talk soon.'

With that, he turns and jogs around the corner of the corridor, disappearing from sight.

'Fuck.' David turns away and slaps his hand against the wall, his jaw clenched.

Lisa chokes out a sob, and Judy's mind is made up. She puts an arm around her daughter's shoulders and steers her towards the doors.

'We'll call you,' she calls, and then the doors swish shut and we're alone.

'She should never have come here.' David's teeth are clenched, his fists balled at his sides. 'After everything that's happened to her, she should've known better.'

I rest a hand on his arm, alarmed by his tone and not wanting to cause a scene in the middle of the reception area. 'Like she said, she panicked. She just wanted to find out what was going on, same as we did.'

He exhales. 'I worry about her health, that's all. And as for that fucking reporter—'

'Wait here,' I say, and then wander over to the nurses' station. 'Excuse me, but we're going to leave. I wondered whether there was someone we could phone later on, or in the morning, to find out how Bec is doing?'

The nurse scribbles a phone number on a page from a complimentary notepad with a pharmaceutical company's name in the top right hand corner, and hands it over.

'Thanks. Will you let her parents know we'll call them?'

'I will if I see them to speak to,' she says noncommittedly, and then lowers her head and goes back to her work.

I wander back to David, a little lost at what to do next.

'Come on. I'll give you a lift back to Bec's so you can pick up your car,' I say after a moment.

I don't wait, I keep walking.

I don't want to stay here any longer.

27

LISA

I NIBBLE at the broken skin around my thumbnail, and eye the woman who is rustling paperwork at her desk.

Dr Heather Bryant is a picture of professionalism; the desk is wide, her laptop open and set to one side while she shoves a stapled document into a manila folder.

I haven't heard from Hayley or David since I saw them at the hospital on Saturday. It's like we've retreated from each other, the shock of Bec's suicide attempt driving a wedge between us because none of us has answers.

Bryant doesn't notice my reticence. She taps the cap of her fountain pen on the lined page of a clean notepad.

'They'll be here any minute,' she says.

I'm not convinced the assurance is for my benefit.

Simon's parents were meant to be here fifteen minutes ago, and I reckon they're going to be a no-show.

I wouldn't blame them, not now. Not now that our lives have been wrung inside out and laid bare for all and sundry to read about.

The story of Simon's death and my life-saving operation made the local TV news last night.

Notwithstanding my new kidney, I feel like I've been punched in the gut.

It's the sense that I've been betrayed. *We've* been betrayed. All of us.

The bastard who accosted me in the hospital yesterday printed another article online about it all, too – and somehow managed to get a photo of me without any of us realising it, despite David's valiant efforts.

I look scared in the photo, and I can see something else in my eyes, too.

Guilt.

The phone on the psychiatrist's desk rings, and she answers it before murmuring, 'Tell them I'll be right there.'

She replaces the receiver and manages a tight smile. 'Mr and Mrs Granger are here. I'll go and get them. Won't be long.'

I watch the door close behind her, then think back to what happened last night, and David's reaction.

It's the first time I've seen him like that in a long time, and I can't get it out of my head. Twice now, in the space of a few hours, he's come to the rescue.

First Bec, then me.

He's always been the quietest out of the five of us, so it's reassuring to see him emerge from the brittle exterior he'd built around himself, and I'm thankful that something good has come out of all this.

The door opens, and Dr Bryant peers around it. She smiles, then pushes it wider.

'Take a seat; Lisa's here already.'

I shuffle to my feet as Simon's mum, Cassandra, appears, her face wan.

Somewhere under the stress lines that crease her forehead is the woman who used to bake brownies on Saturday afternoons when she knew Simon and I would be studying together at his house. Somewhere under the pained gaze she aims at me is a mother who has lost her son, who has no answers, who doesn't know what to believe anymore.

I hold out my hand, and she grasps it between hers. They are warm.

'Oh, Lisa,' she says.

We embrace; and all the pent-up emotions I've tried to bury for the past week threaten to spill. I rub her back as she buries her face in my shoulder, and peer over her head.

Simon's dad, Frank, is watching me with red-rimmed eyes. He nods.

'Let her be, Cass. She must be sore as hell.'

'Oh, bloody hell. Of course.'

Cassandra breaks away, gives me an apologetic smile, and reaches out for Frank's hand.

'We might be more comfortable in the soft chairs,' says Dr Bryant.

She leads the way over to four armchairs that have been arranged in a semi-circle next to the window. A green plant of some sort sits in the middle of a low glass-topped table that I have to shuffle around because it's too close to the chair I've been directed to, and I can't risk moving either the chair or the table in case my wound opens.

Dr Bryant may be one of the hospital's leading

psychiatrists, but she's certainly not au fait with recovery procedures.

I sink into the chair with my back to the window and try to ignore the draught that's filtering down my neck from the air conditioning vent above my head.

Bryant turns to each of us to make sure she has our attention, and then speaks.

'We're here today as you find yourselves in very unusual and traumatic circumstances. It's extremely rare for transplant patients to know their donor's name, and for that I must apologise on behalf of my colleagues. I can assure you that there is a full investigation underway. I'd like to start off by thanking you all to agreeing to this meeting.'

I say nothing, but nod politely.

Frank leans forward. 'We've discussed this, and given how things have worked out, we've told the representative from the NHS Trust that we're not going to pursue it. We may have lost our son, but Lisa is alive because of him.'

Dr Bryant's shoulders relax. 'That's very good of you, thank you. Lisa, would you like to start us off by telling us a little about what you remember about Simon? Your happiest memories?'

I swallow. I didn't expect her to put me on the

spot like this, and, after what Simon put me through in the days and weeks before he died, I'm struggling to think of something.

Cassandra seems to mistake my failure to speak for distress and leans forward to pat my knee. A sad smile crosses her lips.

'You two always used to enjoy doing your homework together, didn't you?'

I nod, silently thanking her. 'Yes. We met in art class and just clicked, really. He was different to the other boys at school – quieter, more reticent. I think that's why we gravitated towards each other.' I take a breath, desperately trying to think of something to add.

'And you used to like the same bands,' Cassandra adds.

The conversation goes on like this – Bryant gives us a question, and we do our best to offer stilted answers, remembering Simon as he could be, not how he actually was.

The bastard who refused to give me one of his kidneys to save my life when all other options were gone.

Finally, after forty minutes, Bryant deems the meeting over and we breathe a collective sigh of relief, sharing shy smiles as we move towards the door.

Frank turns on the threshold, opens his mouth to speak and then frowns.

'Did you want to say something else to Lisa?' says Dr Bryant.

Oh hell. I hold my breath, waiting for him to unleash all the anger and grief he must be feeling, all the frustration that despite the psychiatrist's attempts, none of us has an answer to the questions going around in our heads.

'I saw Simon, the day before he died,' he says, his voice full of wonder. 'I was making a delivery in town to a firm of solicitors.'

'Oh?' I hadn't realised Frank was still working as a courier driver. I'd assumed he'd retired a couple of years ago, like my dad had.

'Yeah.' He scratched his earlobe, his brow knotted. 'He was outside that posh Italian café, sitting at a table with Hayley. I was surprised – it was bloody cold. I hadn't seen her in years, although I know you lot still keep in touch.'

My breath catches in my throat. 'Hayley?'

'Mmm. Looked like they were arguing about something. She got up at one point and was jabbing her finger at him.'

'Do you know what it was about?' I ask.

'No. I was running late, so I went into the solicitors to drop off the parcel before I got a parking ticket. I thought I'd nip over the road and have a quick word with them to see if everything was okay, but when I got back outside they'd both gone.'

And of course, the next day Simon had died.

'I never got the chance to speak to him again,' says Frank.

Cassandra puts her hand on his arm, and then looks at Dr Bryant and me. 'Thank you for today. It isn't easy, but it's good to see you, Lisa. It's good to know something good came out of all this mess.'

I nod, unable to form the words that my mind is screaming.

Why didn't Hayley tell me she and Simon had argued?

What had they been arguing about?

28

HAYLEY

THE COMMON IS SURPRISINGLY busy for a Monday morning.

I scowl at a cyclist as she speeds past, her bright colours quickly fading into the light mist that lifts from the surface of the lake and clings to the trees on the other side of the dirt and gravel path.

Green algae covers the dark water, broken in places by a scrunched up soft drink can, a discarded cigarette packet, a nappy.

I raise my eyes to the left. There is a black plastic bin nailed to a post sunk into a concrete base less than three feet away from the water's edge.

Inhaling, trying to calm my nerves, I shift my gaze back to the lake. Damp fills the air, and with it the sweet aroma of rotting undergrowth and—

Stop it.

I turn my attention to a pair of swans who are gliding past the bench seat before I unbutton my coat and stretch out my legs in front of me. The ankle boots are old, but comfortable, as are the skinny jeans.

I smile; I'm careful with my weight and am pleased I haven't yet been tempted to stuff my face with comfort food over the colder months.

Beyond the lake, the Common stretches away on either side, a green undulating landscape that belies its urban setting.

A siren wails on the breeze that flicks my hair, then falters before being replaced with a loud honk.

A fire engine; nothing to worry about.

A mother shoving a pushchair at the far end of the water leaves the lake shore via a spur in the path, and I lose sight of her between the trees as she heads off in the direction of Hill Lane. The crowds have dispersed now, and I'm alone.

The wind picks up, rustling the reeds and bulrushes to the right of where I sit, sending a waterhen scuttling from within the stalks, her wake rippling across the water before she slows near the middle. The mist recedes, and an azure sky, cloudless for a change, dapples sunlight through the branches of the willow tree above my head.

I close my eyes for a moment, and snuggle into the cashmere scarf around my neck.

The Common was our playground while we were at university. After orientation week, we met up at one of the pubs on the perimeter of the park one Saturday, only to be kicked out two hours later when the elderly landlord decided we were becoming too raucous in his beer garden for his regular clientele.

We purchased bottles of cheap booze and packets of additive-laden snacks from the supermarket at the far end of the Common, and then stumbled our way across the park to a copse of trees on the far side of the lake.

Simon carried a three-quarter size acoustic guitar with him that day, and played it badly – it was what drove the pub patrons up the wall – but here, we'd sat down under the trees with our hastily thrown together picnic and sang and laughed until the stars came out.

As the autumn progressed, our weekend sojourns to the Common became less frequent, shortening with the hours of daylight left to us, rugged up in thick overcoats and the snacks replaced with thermos flasks of hot soup.

And then there was darkness.

Winter.

Death.

I open my eyes.

There is a cemetery at the southern end of the Common; old, unused, going wild. It's guarded by wrought-iron gates between two stone pillars, and inside can be found grave markers for those souls lost at sea on the Titanic. There is an ornamental lake to the north of the Common, but it is to this one near the historic cemetery that I'm drawn.

I keep promising myself that I'll stop coming here, that it's not good for me, but I don't.

I don't know if the others come here: I suspect they do, but it's not like it was during that first term. We no longer congregate here, not after that first winter.

When my mum was still alive, until the cancer finally ripped her from my life three years ago, she asked me why I stayed in the area and visited the lake if I hated it so much. I'd slipped up that day, talking to her.

The old fear had begun to tear at me, creating an unsettling paranoia that I couldn't shake.

'You should find somewhere else to settle,' she'd said. 'The change will do you good.'

Except it wouldn't.

It would make it worse.

I had to stay in the area after finishing university. I had to visit the lake from time to time. We all did, because we had to be sure.

I reach out for my bag that I'd dumped on the bench beside me when I first sat here, and pull out a black leather purse.

Opening the catch, I unfold it, ignoring the debit cards, the credit cards, the store cards, driving licence. I stick my thumb between the inner flap and slide out the photograph, its edges battered from years of receipts, cash and to-do lists being shoved next to it in a hurry.

The last ever Christmas photograph I posed for.

There he is.

Greg.

Standing next to Lisa with his fingers held up like bunny ears behind her, acting like a fool because he was head over heels in love with her, and she didn't have a fucking clue.

Lisa, so naïve. So much younger in some respects than the eighteen years she'd celebrated only weeks before the photograph was taken.

I'm standing between Simon and David, grinning like an idiot with those stupid fake reindeer antlers on my head.

To my left, Simon is playing up to the camera – Bec took this photograph and there was already a growing spark between them at that time.

David is glowering, and if I didn't know better or have this niggling suspicion at the back of my mind then I'd assume he was sulking about the fact that none of our photographs that night, not a single one, was posed with any seriousness.

I suppose it's strange these days to carry a photo around like this. It's something my dad used to do with a fuzzy coloured image of me and my older sister, taken before we started school.

This isn't saved on a phone, not relegated to a social media account that I might use a virtual private network to log into once every few months, and not kept to share with others.

No, this was printed out so we don't forget.

Ever.

29

DAVID

LISA LOOKS exhausted when she opens the front door to her parents' house.

She's wearing a bit of make-up but it does little to disguise the sallowness of her skin, and her eyes are bleary, unfocused.

'David? What are you doing here?'

I move towards her, giving her no option but to step to one side and let me in. 'I was worried about you. I haven't heard from you since we saw you at the hospital. Are you here on your own?'

She closes the door and runs a hand through her hair. 'Mum and Dad always go to the cinema on Tuesday or Saturday afternoons. There's always a cheap matinee performance of the latest release. Some sort of costume drama tosh today, I think.'

She manages a smile, and for a moment I see a hint of the old Lisa. The one who was the life of the party before she got ill.

There's hope, after all.

'Are you okay?' I rip apart the Velcro straps on my cycling shoes, kick them off next to the row of boots and slippers in the hallway, and follow her shuffling footsteps through to the living room. 'You sound a bit out of it.'

'I've just got back from another check-up at the hospital.' She winces as she sits on the sofa and pulls a blanket over her legs. 'And the painkillers are taking a while to kick in.'

That explains the woozy look in her eyes.

'How much longer do you have to be on them?'

'A few more days, and then they put me on a lower dosage. You should see the concoction of meds I'm on; I could start my own pharmacy. Still, if they stop the kidney from rejecting it's worth it. Have you spoken to Bec?'

I sink into one of the armchairs and tap my cycling helmet on my knee. 'They're still not letting her see any visitors apart from immediate family.'

'Christ, it must be bad.'

'She probably just needs a lot of rest. I imagine

with something like that they'll want to do a psych evaluation too, right?'

'I suppose so. For all the good it'll do. Bloody psychiatrists.' She curls her lip, and then a thought seems to occur to her. 'I met with Simon's mum and dad yesterday.'

'Really?' I can't hide my surprise. 'Whose idea was that?'

She frowns. 'The hospital. One of the staff broke with protocol and let slip to my parents who my donor was. They organised a meeting with a psychologist for us – some sort of mitigation strategy, I think, in case Simon's parents were thinking of taking action…'

Her attention wanes, and her gaze moves to the window, the view to the outside world obscured by net curtains and a windowsill cluttered with her mother's awful knick-knacks.

'Lisa?'

'Hmm?'

'How did it go?'

'Oh, all right, I suppose. In the circumstances.' She pulls at an errant thread on the blanket, her eyes lowered. 'It was a bit shit, to be honest. I mean, what are you supposed to say? Sorry your son's dead but, hey, thanks for the kidney.'

I can hear the bitterness in her words; the pain and guilt that spills from her lips.

I dump the cycle helmet on the armchair and move across to where she sits. 'Come on, budge up.'

She shuffles along and I ease next to her, then reach out and wrap my fingers around hers before giving her hand a squeeze.

'It'll get better, I promise.'

'It doesn't feel like it will at the moment. I mean, if I'm still around ten years from now, I'm still going to be thinking about him, aren't I? Wondering what would've happened if he hadn't—'

Died.

Neither of us say the word.

I turn to her. 'What do you mean, if you're around in ten years? You've got a new kidney, haven't you?'

A wistful expression crosses her face, and then she untangles her fingers from mine and rubs at tired eyes. 'A kidney transplant is only a treatment, not a cure. This will buy me time, for sure, but no one knows how long – a year, ten, thirty. But the kidney will definitely fail at some point, and then, if dialysis is still off the table for me...'

'You never said anything.'

'I didn't want to scare any of you.'

'Oh.' I stand up and stretch, easing the kinks from my calf muscles. After a half hour session around the criterium circuit and then riding over here, I'm in danger of cramping up. 'You always got on well with Simon's parents, didn't you?'

'Yes. I used to go around to theirs to do my homework – even before me and Simon were actually going out together.'

'I can't remember the last time I saw them both.'

'Frank's still working as a courier driver. I thought he'd retired a couple of years ago, but he's still out there in all weathers.'

'He always seemed so quiet compared to Cassandra,' I say. 'I can remember a barbecue at theirs – we must've met the rest of you at uni by then because Hayley was around there, too. He seemed content to stay in the background, just listening to the conversation rather than taking part.'

'I think he's probably just shy,' says Lisa. 'Oh, that reminds me—'

I stop stretching and turn to face her. 'What?'

'Frank said he saw Simon arguing with Hayley the day before he died.'

'Where?'

'At that Italian café in the town centre. Frank was delivering a parcel to a solicitor's firm across the street and said he saw them outside.'

'What did Frank say to them?'

'Nothing – he said he was on the clock for the delivery so he had to do that first, and when he came back outside they'd both gone.'

And Simon was dead twenty-four hours later.

'Has Hayley told you what it was all about?'

Lisa shakes her head. 'No, I only found out about it from Frank yesterday. Hayley's been acting weird since Simon died though, haven't you noticed?'

'In what way?'

'She used to have this nervous tic at university when she got stressed out about something. She twiddles the middle earring she wears. She hasn't done that for ages. She did it a lot in our final year, and she's doing it again. I noticed, when she came to see me at the hospital.'

I wander over to where I left my cycle helmet and pick it up before perching on the arm of the chair. 'Look, it's better if you ask her if she's okay when you next see her. I don't want to upset her, not after everything that's happened.'

Lisa lets her head fall back against the cushions.

'Maybe you're right.'

'I am. Perhaps it's something she doesn't want to talk about at the moment.'

'I know, but—' She sits upright, wincing as her abdomen muscles protest.

I move to help her, but she shakes her head.

'I'm okay. I do wonder what they were arguing about though.'

'Well, you probably shouldn't say anything to the police if they ask.'

'What do you mean?'

'Simon's dead and, the day before he dies, Hayley is seen arguing with him. Let's face it – what would that detective, Forbes, make of that if she knew?'

'Jesus.'

She sits, stunned for a moment, and then I see the kindling of an idea in her eyes.

'David? What if the police are right?'

'About what?'

'What if Simon *was* killed? What if he told Hayley he wasn't going to donate a kidney, and she decided to take matters into her own hands after they argued?'

'That's a bit far-fetched, Lisa.'

'It's not though, is it? It's motive.'

THERE's a solitary blackbird pecking at the stunted grass outside the window of the ground floor hospital ward, its wayward zig-zagging progress interrupted from time to time by a grey squirrel darting between the haggard rhododendron bushes.

I've been watching them for the past half an hour, although I haven't been concentrating on whether the bird has managed to find something to eat.

My mind is elsewhere, my jaw clenched as I try to piece together the last twelve days of my life.

No one ever talks about what happens after someone's attempted to kill themselves.

I glance down at the thick gauze dressings

around my forearms and pray that the painkillers kick in soon. My skin and muscles are on fire, ripped to pieces by the cheap kitchen knife I bought in the hardware store down the road from my house the day after I moved in.

I don't remember doing it, but it seems I was pretty accurate.

Another half a centimetre and I'd have severed a major artery, according to the surgeon who stitched me back together and ensured new blood was pumped into my system within moments of the ambulance crew getting here.

She looked down her nose at me as she detailed everything she'd done to save me, making it quite clear without actually using words that she had better things to do than preserve the life of someone who'd done a good job of trying to end it an hour before.

I haven't seen her since.

For the past few days, I've been in the care of the specialist ward nurses who are kind, orderly, soft spoken.

I'm cut off from the outside world, my mobile phone back at the house and my only visitors are my parents whose concern turned to confusion as the days progressed.

I have no answers to their questions. No reassurances to provide.

I turn my back on the window and settle into the chair, my book forgotten on the table in front of me. An exhaustion settles across my shoulders; a familiar sensation that seizes my limbs and makes my eyelids heavy.

Normal, they tell me. All that blood gone, and my body adjusting to the trauma. It'll take time, they say. Rest.

I can't.

There's a memory I can't grasp; a conversation or something I've seen that I know is important.

I recalled it, just before I passed out, and my addled brain is struggling to find it, locked away in my subconscious.

Stuck here, unable to communicate with the outside world until the medical experts reckon they can risk it without me having a second attempt to kill myself, I start to appreciate how Lisa must've felt in the days following her kidney transplant.

Lonely, bored, with too much time on my hands, I understand now why she was so angry that I didn't visit.

Until I told her the truth.

The detective, Forbes, took some persuading.

For a moment, I didn't think she was going to let me go. I thought she'd found something, which was both ridiculous and terrifying.

The police officer – Phillips – looked as exhausted as I felt by the time Forbes escorted me out of the station.

She sneered at me as I walked through the glass double doors and took a deep breath of fresh air.

She's been here, apparently.

One of the nurses, Melanie, told me as she was changing my dressings this morning. I'd been shocked, a sickness silencing me as she'd taped off the ends and patted my shoulder before moving across the room to an elderly man.

I'd been mulling over the news ever since.

Melanie didn't know why Forbes wanted to speak with me. It wasn't a planned visit, that much was clear, and of course the nursing staff are under strict instructions to let me see no one but my parents.

For the moment, I'm safe. I can hide here, recuperate, regroup.

I need a plan, that much is certain.

I rub at my temples. A dull ache persists, one that hasn't left since I woke up after the surgeon had performed her miracles. Dehydration, they've told me. When David found me, there was an empty vodka bottle next to the bath.

I don't remember any of it, of course. For the past six months, and despite trying to convince myself otherwise, my drinking consumption has doubled – no, tripled. I don't know why. It just seems easier sometimes.

I work hard, I rent a scruffy terraced house with a nightmare of a neighbour next door, and I'm broke – I can't afford to get my own place. I watch my friends and work colleagues balance all the problems in their lives, and they seem to sail through.

Me? I go home and open a bottle of wine for starters. And it goes from there.

My gaze falls to my wrists, bound up and on fire from the damage I've done.

I need to fix this. I need to fix me.

How could I have been so stupid? How could I have done this to myself when Simon's parents are mourning the loss of their son? How will the news of this make them feel?

I've told the specialist the hospital has assigned to me that I've never had suicidal thoughts before, and it's true.

So, why now?

I bite my lip, that last memory trying to resurface once more.

I clutch at it, and try to hold on.

—

31

LISA

I PUSH the leftover mash potato and steamed broccoli to one side of my plate, lower my knife and fork, and lean back in my seat.

'Everything all right, love?'

Mum's staring at me, a worried expression in her eyes that I hope she loses as soon as I'm well enough to move out. I've spoken to my former boss at the graphic design agency, and I've got my old job back there whenever I'm able to start.

The constant fussing is wearing me down, and even though I know Mum means well, we were never meant to share a confined space again once I'd bought my flat and moved out.

I bite back the first retort that reaches my lips, and instead force a smile.

'Just tired, Mum. That's all.'

'I expect that meeting with Simon's parents took more out of you than you realised,' Dad says. He reaches over, grabs my plate and scrapes my leftovers onto his, then adds a dollop of brown sauce to the potato and demolishes it with gusto.

I take my empty plate from him, slide Mum's across the table from her and begin to stack the dishwasher.

'Don't overdo it,' she warns. 'You're not meant to be lifting anything heavy.'

'I think I'll be okay doing this. I can't sit around doing nothing anymore.'

Besides, I'm feeling better. Physically, at least.

I took the last of the strong painkillers yesterday. I know I told David I had to take them for another three days, but after his revelation about Hayley and Simon I need a clear mind. I'm making do with anti-inflammatories from the supermarket, enough to keep the last of the bruising at bay.

I have a purpose now, a way ahead of me.

Something to do.

The light is waning outside the window above the sink, and as I pull the blind down I wonder what Hayley is doing right now.

I've been wracking my memory since David's

visit whether she mentioned anything to me before Simon died and I got rushed into hospital. I can't imagine what she might have been arguing about with him. Surely, as one of her closest friends at university and since, she'd have confided in me?

Why hadn't she? What was she hiding?

I move away from the sink to find Mum and Dad watching me.

'Everything okay, love? You were miles away for a moment,' says Mum.

'I'm fine. I'm going to head upstairs and read for a while.'

'Shout down if you need anything.'

I take my time going up to the spare room, my steps heavy.

As I push open the door and sit on the edge of the bed, I pull my laptop towards me and flip open the lid. I ignore David's advice and scroll through the larger newspaper sites, avoiding anything local in case there are more revelations from Stella Barrett and her colleagues. Instead, I work my way through trashy entertainment news and film reviews, trying to create some white noise to counteract the tumbling thoughts going around in my head.

My hand freezes over the keyboard as I realise

with a jolt that the four of us haven't been together since the day Simon died.

Somehow, we've missed each other; one of us has always been inaccessible. I frown. If Hayley and David were close enough that she confided in him, why didn't they visit me at the hospital together? Hayley knows he doesn't like driving, and she would've had to go past his place on the way to see me.

Bec said the police didn't come to see her until Wednesday, so where was she on Monday and Tuesday? Why didn't she get in touch?

And, most of the time, David works from home, so why didn't he show up until the Wednesday?

What were the three of them up to? Where had they been?

I growl through my teeth and close the laptop with a slap. I've got to stop doing this.

I've got to stop finding reasons to doubt what my friends are telling me. All the trauma from the transplant operation, the painkillers, new medication, being here at Mum and Dad's – it's taking its toll on me.

After all, I've seen them since, separately. And I saw Hayley and David at the hospital together, even if we weren't allowed to speak with Bec.

I sigh, and shove the laptop away.

If Hayley has something on her mind, as David says, well, I'll let her know I'm here when she needs me if she wants someone to talk to about whatever's troubling her.

There's nothing to worry about.

32

HAYLEY

I REST my hands on the kitchen worktop and close my eyes as my vision wavers and a rushing sound fills my ears.

It's not the first time it's happened, but it's the first time it's left me feeling so weak.

I blink, then move to the sink and fill a glass with cold water, my hand shaking.

I've barely eaten for days, not since David found Bec and we rushed to the hospital.

I can't. Food is tasteless and I find myself choking when I try to swallow. I'm just about holding it together enough to run the business. I've cancelled all the meetings I had planned for the next ten days, and hope to hell this passes.

It's all I can do to process the timesheets and

invoices to keep my cleaning staff paid on time. I can't let them down – they have families to feed, kids in school, lives of their own. They depend on me.

The reporter – the one who accosted Lisa at the hospital – has been leaving messages on my phone. It's only a matter of time before he turns up on the doorstep, and then what?

I have nothing to say to him, but that doesn't make me feel better. After all, they printed lies about Bec, and no one questioned it. Not one of them thought to ask if what was printed was the truth.

They never do.

I drain the glass in four deep gulps.

The giddiness wears off and I stumble back to the dining area, collapse into my chair and wiggle the mouse to wake up the laptop screen.

There are no new stories about us. The damage has been done, and the journalists have new prey. We are yesterday's news now.

So, why does he persist in trying to speak to me? Has he found out something new?

I reach out for my phone and dial the number for the hospital. After a few moments, I'm put through to Bec's ward.

They still won't let me talk to her, and because I'm not family they won't give me an update either, other than to say she is progressing well.

I hang up.

I scroll through my contacts list, and my thumb hovers over two familiar names.

I've known Bec's parents since I was twenty, but I'm too scared to talk to them.

I don't know what to say. I've never been good at this, this business of offering hope or condolences or whatever it is I should be doing.

Instead, I'm numb.

People think I'm cold because of that, that inability to express sympathy or empathy. The truth is, I've learned to shut myself off from it all. It's the only form of protection I know. Nothing else works.

I wish I hadn't argued with Simon.

There, I've said it.

If somebody finds out about that, it's all over for me. No one will believe me. It won't matter what I say.

I knew I should never have agreed to meet him, not there. Not somewhere so public, in view of everyone. But that's how he wanted it, wasn't it?

I had to agree. I needed to speak to him.

I had to let him know.

But our last words to each other were spoken in anger. I shouldn't feel guilty, I know I shouldn't, because he was a conniving bastard who used people. If it wasn't for the others, I'd have severed all ties with him years ago, especially after—

Stop it.

I straighten my shoulders and take a deep breath before pushing the chair backwards.

I shower first, taking my time, scrubbing grease from my hair and combing through a thick conditioning treatment that fills the bathroom with the sweet scent of watermelon.

Once dry, I stand in front of my wardrobe, then select a bright-red cashmere sweater that will go some way to offset the pallor of my skin, and pair it with black trousers.

I have to do something before it's too late. Before they suspect something.

My phone rings, and my heart misses a beat.

I wonder why the police haven't interviewed me again, and then chastise myself. They probably will, they just haven't yet. I can't imagine that detective – Forbes – giving up until she gets to the bottom of what happened in the escape room, and why Simon died.

I'm certainly not going to help her.

The phone has stopped ringing, and as I listen to the voicemail message he's left, I realise I don't have a choice anymore.

I delete the message and open the recent calls log, my finger poised over the familiar number.

Before I can talk myself out of it, I press the call button.

33

LISA

I RAISE my hand above my head and stretch, careful not to pull the stitches that are healing well.

I'm putting on weight, thanks in part to the drugs I'm on to make sure my body doesn't reject my new kidney, and my mind is clearer than it has been for weeks. Now that I've stopped taking the potent concoction of painkillers, I can think straight.

I've decamped from my old bedroom to the kitchen table. Hunching over my laptop on the bed is doing no good for my abdomen and I needed a change of scenery – however small.

Dad's out with an old work colleague of his, and Mum's dusting her collection of china in the living room so I savour the peace and quiet.

My gaze returns to the laptop screen, and to the message I've received this morning.

It's from somebody I knew vaguely at university, one of those tentative friendships that didn't quite fully blossom but meant that we stayed in touch over the years.

Charlotte now works in the diplomatic service, living in Berlin with a German husband and their two children.

She's known about my illness over the past twelve months, so she wrote a couple of days ago seeking an update on my prognosis. I emailed back, telling her about Simon's death and the impact it's had on all of us these past two weeks, and now her response has my heart racing.

Charlotte was the only person I could think of that would be discreet. As far as I know, she doesn't keep in touch with the rest of them. Just me.

I shan't tell David I've contacted Charlotte. He'd be livid with me for a start for talking about our lives with someone he'd view as a complete stranger.

Hayley, I'm not sure about. I think she knows more than she would have me believe. And, of course, none of us are allowed to see Bec at the moment, so I can't ask her.

'I do hope you manage to rally together to get through this,' says Charlotte in her email. 'But then, you always did. No one could ever understand why you all drifted away from the rest of us that winter. You went from being the life of the party to being almost cloistered away. We used to joke that the five of you had formed a cult or something. I was too in awe of some of you to dare to ask what had happened, especially after Greg disappeared without a trace.'

I write back, making some pithy comment that I know what she means, and then turn the conversation back to Charlotte's career. I figure talking about herself and her achievements would make her think my reply is nothing to worry about.

The doorbell rings as I send the email, and I sit stock-still.

Is it the journalist? Has he decided to come here having failed to get a quote from me at the hospital?

My throat dries, making it hard to swallow, and then—

'Lisa? It's Hayley here to see you.'

'Be right there.'

'We're in the front room.'

Hayley?

I close the laptop, shove it next to Mum's

housekeeping magazine and tidy away the paperwork strewn across the table.

Has she somehow found out that I'm delving into our past, and that I know she was seen arguing with Simon?

I hurry down the hallway, pausing to check my face in the mirror at the bottom of the stairs, and I'm relieved to see that I don't look as worried as I feel. At least I have some colour in my cheeks now, and that vacant dullness in my eyes has all but gone.

I can hear Hayley and my mum talking in the living room, and they pause mid-sentence as I push the door open.

'Here she is,' says Mum. She's got a duster in her hand, and gives me a smile. 'I'll let you two catch up while I get on with my chores.'

Hayley and I share a smile as she leaves the room. Mum hasn't changed at all since we were at university, and the familiarity helps to alleviate some of the panic threatening to bubble to the surface.

As I take a seat in one of the armchairs, I notice the new gold hoop earrings Hayley is wearing. The three studs are gone, and I wonder if she realised that I'd noticed the nervous tic when she visited me at the hospital.

'I thought you might want some company,'

she says. 'I spoke with the hospital this morning, and although they couldn't tell me much, they did say that Bec is well on the mend.'

'That's fantastic news. Do they know when she might be released?'

'No, or if they do, they're not telling me. I guess we'll just have to wait until they do and she gets in touch.' She looks down at her hands. 'I keep wondering whether I should phone her parents but the thing is, I don't know what to say. After everything that happened with Simon and you, I just—'

'I know. The longer we leave it though, the more awkward it's going to get, isn't it? Do you know if David has spoken to them since you saw them at the hospital, given he was the one that saved her?'

'No – I haven't heard from him since that night.'

'Oh.' I lean back in the chair, and decide to try something. 'Everything seemed so much simpler when we were at university, didn't it?'

'What do you mean?'

'I don't know. All of this, with Simon dying and everything else. That last year, all I could envisage was getting out and getting a job – not this. What about you?'

She chokes out a bitter laugh, and eyes her wristwatch before pushing herself to her feet. 'I couldn't wait to see the back of the place.'

34

LISA

I'M STARTING to lose count of the appointments I've had at the hospital since being discharged after the transplant.

I've spent Thursday morning having blood tests taken and urine samples procured, and now I'm sitting in a waiting room watching an American soap opera on a television that hangs above the pharmacy counter while I wait for my prescription.

In between the fractured love lives of who I suppose must be the main characters, I watch the staff dole out drugs and medical aids, a constant stream of patients keeping them busy.

Beside me, David flicks through a cycling magazine he found in a stack on a table in the corner, muttering under his breath at the articles.

'There's no way I'd pay that much for a carbon fork.'

He offered to bring me here, to wait and keep me company and for that, I'm grateful. Mum and Dad have seen enough of hospitals these past twelve months to last them a lifetime, and to be honest I needed to get out of the house – without them.

I scroll through the property app on my phone and flag another one-bedroom terrace I've spotted on the outskirts of town. It's cheap enough that with a small loan from my parents, I'll be able to buy it outright and it's far enough away to regain my independence without completely alienating them.

It's time to move on. Time to live my life again.

The middle-aged balding man who's been sitting opposite us is called, and we have the room to ourselves now.

David scoots across the room, snatches up the television remote and flicks through the channels until he finds a nature programme. He shrugs as he returns to his chair.

'Better than the alternative, I suppose.'

'I was enjoying that.'

'You're kidding.'

I smile, and he gently slaps my arm.

'Did the police tell you how Simon died?' he says, dropping the remote onto a table next to his chair.

'No.' My interest is piqued. I lean forward. 'Have they told you?'

He nodded.

'How come they didn't tell me?'

'You've only just had a kidney transplant, Lisa. Maybe they were waiting until you recovered.'

I wrinkle my nose. 'No. That doesn't make sense. They haven't waited to question me, have they? So why not tell me what happened?'

'Doesn't   it   contravene   patient-donor confidentiality or something?'

I snort. 'Oh, come on. All that's gone out the window, hasn't it?'

A silence falls between us, and I fold my arms across my chest.

Eventually, he speaks, his voice low. 'He hit his head, Lisa. That's all. He had too much to drink at lunchtime, and tripped.'

'Is that what they said to you?'

'It's what happened. I don't know why they've been questioning you. I don't know why Bec was taken in to speak with them. They were probably just making sure.'

'Then why was Hayley seen arguing with him?'

He rolls his eyes. 'Leave it alone, Lisa, please. How do you think Hayley will feel if she knows you're sneaking around behind her back?'

'I was only interested. I thought—' I lower my eyes and try to ignore the tight sensation in my chest that is building. I'm hurt by his words, but I realise he's got a point.

What right do I have to poke around in my friend's private life?

'Am I losing the plot, David?'

'I don't know. Are you?'

I shake my head and turn my gaze to the corridor beyond the door.

Two porters hurry past, one pushing an empty wheelchair while the other has some sort of trolley laden with cleaning materials and medical supplies.

It's all so normal out there.

David closes the magazine, crosses the room to drop it onto the collection piled up on a bookcase near the door, and then walks back. He stops in front of me, brushes my hair from my face and plants a light kiss on my forehead.

'I think all those drugs have got you thinking crazy thoughts,' he says. He smiles, then squeezes my shoulder as the pharmacist calls my name. 'Come on. Let's get you home.'

35

DAVID

THANK CHRIST, Lisa is going to be all right.

My hands are shaking as I take her home after the appointment, but for once it's not because I lack confidence driving and it's rush hour; it's the fact that her consultant has informed her that everything went as well as it could. She's over the first hurdle in her road to recovery.

I glance across at her.

She's smiling as she watches the world go by her window, her hands clasped in her lap and her shoulders relaxed.

I swear she almost skipped back into the waiting room after the appointment. I haven't seen her that happy in months.

She gave me a fierce hug, and we stood there for

a moment as all the stress of the past year, the loss of Simon, everything slipped away.

'I think we should have a celebratory drink,' I say now.

She turns to face me, her eyes wide. 'Do you think I should?'

'I'm sure you can have a small glass of wine. We should celebrate. This is good news, isn't it?'

A flash of guilt crosses her features, and then it's gone. Her mouth twitches.

'I could murder a Shiraz.'

Her hand flies to her mouth before she's finished speaking, and I reach across and pat her knee. 'I know. I know.'

She recovers, and then says, 'Do you want to give Hayley a call?'

God, no.

'Probably best not to,' I say. 'We'll just have a quiet one, and then I'll get you home. I imagine your mum and dad will want to hear how you got on as soon as possible, right?'

'True.'

She goes back to staring out the window, and I wonder if I've made an error in judgement, and then she turns back to me.

'I never thanked you.'

'Thank me?'

'For all this. Driving me around, coming to see me in hospital and at home.'

'It's the least I could do. You'd have done the same for me, right?'

'Yes.' She shuffles in her seat, resting her head against it and angling her legs sideways.

'You okay?'

'Just getting comfy. My abdomen gets sore still if I sit in one position for too long.'

'How long did your specialist say you have to wait until you can start moving around more?'

'Another six weeks before I can do anything strenuous, but I can start walking every day to build up my strength.'

'Maybe you could come cycling with me when you're ready and it warms up? There are some great routes around here.'

She laughs. 'Come on. Don't you remember what I was like at uni? You're talking to the person who fell off her bike braking at the zebra crossing opposite the business school. God, I've never been so embarrassed in all my life.'

'I could get you some training wheels.'

It's great to hear her laughing again. It reminds me what it used to be like, the five of us taking the piss out of each other. Before life got in the way.

Before death got in the way.

The road winds through a wooded area, and then follows a shallow incline into a picturesque village. The pub is on the corner, past a Norman church. It's a few miles out of the city, but worth the detour. It's a gorgeous spot – and quiet.

'Look, I'll drop you outside while I park the car round the back. Save you walking.'

'Okay, thanks.'

She plucks her bag from the footwell and eases out the car once I've pulled to the kerb.

By the time I've found a parking space behind the sixteenth-century pub and pushed open the thick wooden door into the bar, she's chatting to the landlord and two businessmen who are nursing pints of bitter.

The sweet aroma of burning logs from the open fire fills the air, and I shrug off my coat as the warmth begins to take effect.

Lisa turns as I join her, and smiles up at me.

'This was a great idea.'

'Good.' I catch the landlord's attention. 'Half a bitter, and a small glass of Shiraz, please.'

I pay and then we wander over to a table that's

next to the window, pale sunlight streaming through the glass. There's a window seat upholstered in soft fabric, and we opt to sit there rather than on the hard chairs on the other side of the table.

Lisa props herself up with some cushions and reaches out for the glass of wine.

'Cheers,' I say, clinking my drink against hers. 'Here's to a continued speedy recovery. And training wheels.'

'Cheers.' She takes a tentative sip, then sets the glass down. 'Oh, I've missed that.'

'What's next for you, then? Now that your health is on the up?'

'I've been looking at houses.'

'To buy, or rent?'

'To buy. I did all right selling my place last year when all this kicked off but I can't wait to get out of Mum and Dad's place.' A wry smile crosses her features. 'They've been great, they really have, but—'

'You need your own space.'

'Yeah. I need my independence back now.'

I sip the beer, mulling over her words.

'If you need a hand going to look at places, I can help.'

'You've already done too much, really. I don't

want to take the piss and keep asking you to help me.'

'I don't mind, honest. It'll be a few weeks before you'll be allowed to drive anyway, won't it?'

She takes another sip of the wine, then, 'I suppose so. What about your work? Won't they mind?'

I think of the architectural practice in town where I'm cooped up five days a week when I can't convince them to let me work from home, and then shake my head. 'I haven't used much annual leave these past twelve months. They can't stop me from taking some time off. Safer, too for you. I don't like the idea of you looking at places on your own.'

'If you're sure?'

'Positive. Just call me when you have something lined up to look at, and we'll go. It'll be good if there are two of us as well. We'll probably come up with different questions for the agent, and it might help with the negotiating if they think they're up against two of us.'

'True. Okay, thanks.' She puts down the glass and picks up her handbag. 'Back in a minute.'

'Everything okay?' I can't stop the alarm in my voice. After all, this was my idea. What if the wine has done something? What if—

'I need to pee.'

She winks, scoots across the window seat, and makes her way towards the ladies' toilets.

The two men at the bar turn to watch her as she passes, and I smile.

The Lisa Ashton I know is back, that much is certain.

36

LISA

I SHINE the torch into the far recesses of the garage, and curse under my breath as I realise the box I want is, of course, the one at the back.

Placing the torch on top of an old filing cabinet that Dad uses to store his car cleaning kit and fishing tackle, I squint in the remaining light from the single bulb that dangles from a wire in the rafters, and wipe my dust-streaked hands on my jeans.

I know I shouldn't be in here. I know I shouldn't risk pulling a muscle or worse, but there's something in that box.

Something that fills me with hope – and fear.

Hope, because I desperately need some answers for the questions that keep me awake at night.

Fear, because I'm scared what those answers might be.

I sneeze, but bite back the twist of pain. I need to be left alone.

I glance over my shoulder to the door, but no one appears. Mum and Dad are watching a true crime documentary on TV, and they think I'm upstairs reading.

As if I could concentrate on words spilling across a page right now. This is all I've been thinking about in the hours since David dropped me back here.

I glare at the boxes.

There are eight in total, each about the size of one of those old style tea chests. There are two stacked one on top of the other to my right, another two stacked on my left. In front of me, under a window that would look out over the back garden in daylight if it weren't for the thick cobwebs strewn across the panes, are the other four boxes.

It is the one on the far left that I need to get to. The one on which I wrote "Misc Stuff" in thick black felt-tip pen all those months ago when I sold my flat – my sanctuary – and moved back here.

I take a step back as plastic rustles, then stoop to pick up the black bin liner.

Deciding that if I was going to come out here and rummage through the boxes, I reasoned with myself that I should make a start sorting through all this. If I was going to move out, going to move on with my life, then some of the old things I'd clung to should probably be donated to a charity – or thrown away.

I packed these boxes in a hurry.

The flat was sold quickly; I hadn't the health or the time left to haggle for a better price although I'd done all right out of it, and the new owners wanted to move in within six weeks.

I refused help from my parents, David, Bec, anyone who offered to pack my things for me.

It was painful, to accept my ailing health and with it, my independence.

Packing my belongings, admitting defeat in not being able to care for myself any longer, was a way for me to mourn.

I sniff, and then eye the box of Misc Stuff once more.

'Right,' I say, with more determination than I feel.

My voice sounds loud in this tight, enclosed space but Mum and Dad won't hear.

The garage is separate from the house, accessed

across a concrete paved path that runs from the back door of the house down to the garden shed, a clothes line following its length.

I turn and survey the two boxes to my left. If I can sort through the contents of these, lifting out a bit at a time, I'll be able to get to the one I need at the back there without having to climb over or trying to lift it towards me.

I square my shoulders. No doubt my bravado has been aided by the second glass of wine I decided to have earlier with David at the pub, but I'm determined now.

I push against the top box and am relieved to find it isn't full. I take a deep breath, then shuffle it towards me. Although the muscles in my abdomen protest, it's not as bad as I thought.

I peer around the sides of it until I can see my scrawl: "Linen".

Easy.

I let the box crash to the floor, safe in the knowledge nothing will be broken. One down, one to go.

I shove the box of pillowcases, bath towels and duvet covers to one side and peer at the side of the second box.

"Ornaments".

Bollocks. This will be a while. There's absolutely no chance of lifting it, and it's going to take ages to go through everything inside.

I use my house key to slice through the tape that holds the lid in place and then start to work my way through each bundle of coloured tissue paper. A lot of this will go in the charity bag: kitsch knick-knacks from holidays abroad, mementoes from gift shops that I'd picked up from doing walks along the coast path between West Bay and Lyme Regis one summer, and vases I no longer like the look of. Then there are the shells, sea glass, and stones I thought were interesting at the time. These I will take outside and dot around Mum's garden tomorrow when it's light.

An hour later, I lean against the filing cabinet and wipe sweat from my eyes.

The black bin liner is now half full, and an exhilaration fills me as I realise I did this. Two weeks ago, I didn't have the energy to even contemplate anything like it.

I check my watch. It's half past nine, and Mum and Dad's TV programme will end soon. I need to get a move on.

I know I don't want their help with this. What's

in that box at the back under the window is something I have to find on my own.

I push away from the cabinet and run my hand across the top of a half-full wine rack as I make my way to the back of the garage once more.

Nearly there.

My legs shake as I pull the box of remaining ornaments across the concrete floor, and I know I'm reaching my physical limits tonight. The after-effects of a general anaesthetic, the trauma my body has been through, and the cocktail of drugs I must take for the rest of my life – not to mention the wine earlier – are taking their toll, but I won't give up.

I can't give up. Not yet.

The key slips from my grip as I move to slice the tape across the box full of "Misc Stuff", and falls down the side next to the wall with a tinkle of brass on concrete.

'No!'

I'm horrified. I need that key. There are no scissors on the shelves over by the door, and Dad doesn't keep his knives with the bait and tackle supplies. I wouldn't know where else to search for something sharp amongst all the clutter in here.

I don't want to return to the house in case Mum

sees me and asks what I'm doing moving boxes around in my state.

I snatch up the torch and shine it at my feet, then move the beam to the left as something catches my eye near the bottom of the box.

Thank God.

The key protrudes from the box and the wall, just enough that I can pinch the end between my fingers and drag it out.

I try not to imagine the spiders that must be behind there as I dust a cobweb from the key and then rip it along the tape before I risk dropping it again.

Sliding the key back into my jeans pocket, I pull open the flaps of the box and peer inside.

It's exactly what I'd hoped.

I had a two-bedroom flat, and used the smaller front upstairs room as an office. I say office, but the space was mostly a receptacle for things that didn't belong elsewhere or I didn't want to leave in the damp garage at the back of the building with an old roll-up door and a dodgy lock.

These items used to jostle for space on one of two squat bookshelves that had been in that room.

As I kneel and reach inside, my fingers wrap around the first of the paperbacks I'd tossed on top of everything else as an afterthought, and then some framed certificates – including my bachelor's degree.

I frown as a memory resurfaces – it's not what I was expecting, and I sit back on my heels in surprise, still clutching the framed degree certificate.

I run my gaze over the bright colours of the embossed coat of arms, the signatures flourishing above names I've forgotten, and the honorary award I'd achieved through sheer determination and effort.

I remember I lost myself in my studies after that first winter.

I put the frame to one side and keep rummaging.

It's in here. I know it is.

Five minutes later, trying not to get distracted by the other forgotten treasures that I discover, I open a manila file that was once green and is now faded. It has an old coffee stain on the front of it.

My heart rate spikes as I leaf through the newspaper cuttings from my graduation ceremony. The local press photographer managed to capture the moment Bec and I had caught each other's mortarboards as they'd tumbled from the air and we were grinning at each other maniacally, but it's the newspaper clipping underneath this one that makes me gasp.

I was right.

It's yellowed with age — after all, it's over seven years old — but the black bold headline is as shocking now as it was then.

UNIVERSITY   STUDENT   MISSING. POLICE APPEAL FOR INFORMATION.

37

HAYLEY

He's got a bounce in his step as he winds his way between the tables in the café over to where I sit.

I picked somewhere different for today's meeting. Somewhere that I'm not known. I'm hoping the change of scenery works for my nerves.

He leans down, kisses me on the cheek, and then sinks onto the seat next to me and reaches out for the menu.

'What are you having?'

'I haven't decided yet.'

'Been waiting long?'

'No, I only got here fifteen minutes ago. I thought I'd get a table at the back so we can talk in private. It's busier than I thought it'd be.'

He looks up from the extensive list of cooked

breakfast options and casts his gaze around the café, then back to me. 'Paranoid?'

I glare at him. 'How come you're so happy?'

'Nothing.'

I hate this, this sing-song tone in his voice that means he knows something I don't, and he knows in turn that it riles me. I bite back the retort that is already forming and instead look up as a waitress wanders over.

'Ready to order?'

He doesn't offer to let me go first.

'I'll have the full English and a cappuccino, please.' He smiles at her, all charm and swagger. 'And could I have an extra sausage?'

'No problem, love. And for you?'

'Eggs Benedict, please, and coffee – black.'

She whisks the menus from our hands, assures us the food will be with us as soon as possible – there's a lull in activities in the kitchen – and then leaves us to it.

I have to tell him. I have to let him know. That's what we agreed.

'That police officer, Forbes, came to see me again yesterday.'

His head snaps round to face me, his ogling of

the group of girls near the front window forgotten. 'Why?'

'She said she was just following up. Routine enquiries. I don't know.'

He holds up a hand to stop me as the waitress approaches with our coffees.

We make the appropriate noises of thanks, add sugar and wait until she's out of earshot.

He leans forward, his voice low. 'What did she ask you?'

'Whether I'd been to see Lisa since she left hospital. What we spoke about, what our friendship was like.'

'What did you say?'

'I told her the truth, didn't I? We've known each other since the first year at university. Studied marketing and business subjects together. Blah, blah, blah.'

His eyes narrow. 'What else did she want to know?'

'They got the post-mortem report.'

'I know.'

I don't expect that, and I'm caught off guard. 'How did you know?'

'I have my ways.'

'Has she spoken to you as well?'

'Not yet.'

'So, how do you know?'

Shit. The waitress is heading back our way, carrying two plates laden with hot food, and the moment is lost. I unwrap the cutlery, spread the paper napkin over my trousers and add a generous sprinkling of black pepper to the hollandaise sauce.

He's already tucking into his breakfast with aplomb, shovelling the food into his mouth as if it's the last meal he's going to get this week.

My top lip curls at the sight.

Halfway through our meal, I try again. 'They say he died of a heart attack. I thought he just hit his head.'

'Yeah.'

'I didn't know he had a heart problem, did you?'

'No. Maybe he didn't know. A lot of people don't.'

'I suppose so.'

I can't eat any more. My stomach tightens, and I know it's because this is the first real food I've had in too long. I need to be careful, otherwise I'm going to make myself sick. I lower the knife and fork to the plate, dab my lips with the napkin and then toss it over the leftover food and lean back in my seat while he finishes his.

'Do you think they'll leave us alone now, then?' I finally say. 'Now that they know?'

He scrapes the last of the tomato sauce from the plate with his knife, licks it and then shoves the plate to one side and folds his arms on the table, his hands wrapped around his coffee cup. 'Probably. Not a lot else they can do, is there?'

'Then why did she come to see me?'

'I don't know. You were the one she spoke to. What did she say when you asked her?'

'Just that she was updating their report, and that she wanted to check some details.'

'Such as?'

'What time we got to the escape room, where we'd been before that.'

'Did you tell her?'

'Of course I did. I said we'd been to the Ragamuffin Bar for a few drinks before we walked over the road to the escape room.'

'Did she ask anything else?'

'No.'

He drains the coffee, signals the waitress over, then asks for another. He watches as she gathers up the plates.

'Have you spoken to Bec's parents?' I ask when she's gone.

'No. Why would I?'

'I wondered, that's all.'

'Why? Want me to ask them if she's said anything? Wondering if she's going to tell everyone what you've done?'

I drop my cup into the saucer with a clatter, chuck a twenty pound note on the table and grab my bag before pushing back my chair, then bend down and shove my face next to his.

'Fuck you, David. I know what you did.'

38

LISA

ANOTHER FOLLOW-UP APPOINTMENT. One more blood test. One more consultant to see this week, and then that's it.

I don't have to come back until next week.

Four whole days without the stench of disinfectant, the squeak of rubber-soled shoes on tiled floors, the sight of all these sick people.

I can sense freedom, despite the regular appointments I will have to keep for the next three months. My heart rate quickens every time I think of the future.

My future. My plans.

I smile as Dr Clark reads through the latest report and reiterates what three other doctors already told me last week.

'So,' he says, scribbling another prescription and handing it to me, 'you need to pick up these from the pharmacy counter on your way out, and then we'll see you in a few days to check on progress.'

He pats my back as he opens the consulting room door for me.

I pause on the threshold and hold out my hand. 'Thank you. For everything. I realise I'm lucky, that not all of your patients get this far, but I want you to know how much I appreciate what you and your team have done for me.'

He seems taken aback, and for a fleeting moment I wonder if I'd said something wrong but then he clasps my hand between his own, and smiles.

'Every success helps us through the others,' he says. 'It's why we do this.'

We part, with me agreeing to phone him if I've got any concerns, and then I follow the winding corridor back through the hospital, back towards the exit.

The pharmacy counter has a queue eight deep, but I can't get these drugs from our local chemist, not without a twenty-four-hour wait, and I have to start taking these today.

I resign myself to shuffling forward behind a

young couple with a new-born baby, the mother's face drawn and pale. I hope to hell the baby's okay and they're only here for routine medicine. Headache pills, maybe.

'Lisa?'

I turn at the sound of my name, and my jaw drops open.

Bec's mother is hurrying towards me, her arms outstretched while Derek, Bec's dad, hovers in the background. He holds up a hand in greeting as Sue envelopes me in a bear hug.

'You're looking well, love. Good to see you.'

Relief floods through me; I thought they'd be angry with me, that they thought I'd abandoned their daughter, that I hadn't been there to stand up for her.

'Lisa.' Derek stoops to kiss my cheek. I'd forgotten how damn tall he was – I always thought he resembled an oak tree when I first met him, but his kind-hearted nature soon put me at ease.

'Have you been to see Bec?'

'Yes. We've been here every day, trying to help her cope with everything.'

Any other mother would be traumatised by what had happened to her daughter – mine would be – but Sue seems more pragmatic.

'They haven't let us yet,' I tell them. 'How is she?'

'Getting there,' says Derek. He's not as stoic as his wife, and his voice wobbles. 'But she's a good kid. She'll come through it.'

Sue slips her fingers through his. 'They're very pleased with her progress. I think she simply hit rock bottom, and didn't know how to cope.'

'I feel so bad I couldn't be there for her.'

Sue shakes her head. 'How could you be? You were recovering from a transplant. Don't be silly. Bec would've known that. I think this has been building up for a while, to be honest. That's what the psychiatrist thinks, anyway. Too much stress, he said. And then, what with Simon's death …'

She sighs, and Derek puts his hand around her shoulders, drawing her near. 'You can go in and see her, if you want.'

'Really?'

'They reckon she'll be able to come home at the weekend, so they're lifting visiting restrictions. They probably think it'll ease her into talking about it… about what happened.'

'If you wander along there now, you can probably see her before visiting hours are over,' says Sue. 'She'd love to see you.'

I think back to our last conversation, the strange way Bec acted before she hurried from the house, and I wonder if Sue's assumption is correct.

'Okay,' I say. I check over my shoulder but the queue has hardly moved. 'I'll go now. I can stop by here on my way out.'

'Wonderful.' Sue beams at me, then Derek. 'We'd best be going. We only put three hours on the car, and we're already ten minutes over. Good to see you, Lisa.'

'You too.'

I wander across to the reception desk, check where to find Bec's ward and then follow the green line painted on the ceiling up three floors and towards the back of the hospital.

It's more peaceful here.

There's none of the bedlam that fills the ground floor, no one dashing around to be somewhere they should've been half an hour ago, and a calmer atmosphere lingers all around me.

I scan the index for the floor outside the lift doors, and set off along a corridor lined on one side with floor-to-ceiling windows that overlook the car park on one side and landscaped gardens on the other. It's all new, this wing. I remember seeing the articles online about some dignitary or other attending an opening ceremony a year or so ago.

I see Bec before she spots me.

She's in an armchair next to a window at the far end of a room that resembles a care home – there are various armchairs dotted around the edges, all of which are empty at the moment.

She looks up as I near. 'Did you see Mum and Dad downstairs?'

'Yes. I thought your mum was going to hug all the air out of my lungs.'

That makes her smile, at least.

I pull out a chair next to her, eyeing the bandages that cover her wrists.

She notices, and holds up her hands. 'I reckon I'm on the same painkillers as you.'

'Are they working?'

She nods, drops her hands to her lap, and shoots me a sideways look. 'How are you?'

'That was my line.'

'I asked first.'

'All going well, as far as they can tell at the moment. I met with my consultant earlier. They've changed my medication again. That's when I saw your mum and dad downstairs.'

'Did they seem okay?'

'Yes. Worried about you, but grateful that you're okay.' There's no easy way to do this. 'Why'd you do it, Bec?'

'This?'

'Yeah.'

'I don't know. I guess I felt I didn't have much of a choice anymore.' She picks at a loose thread on one of the bandages. 'Enough about me. So, your transplant worked, then?'

'Yes, seems so.'

'What's next for you, then?'

I tell her my plans for buying my own place, going back to work when I'm recovered. Normal things.

'That's good. That's really good.'

She sounds genuine. I shuffle in my seat. 'Can I ask you something?'

'What?'

'Why did you and Simon split up?'

Her shoulders sag. 'I suppose it'll all come out now anyway. He owed me money. A lot of money. When we first got together, he was investing in a new software application. One of his ex-colleagues was leading the project, and Simon got involved. He wanted to be in it at the beginning, not just as a developer but as a vested business partner. He didn't have enough money of his own, so he asked me and said he'd pay me back within six months. I stupidly agreed.'

'What happened?' I ask, dread crawling in my stomach.

'I asked him back in July when I could expect my money. He stalled for a while, saying he was saving for the wedding next year. I gave up waiting six weeks ago. That's when he told me there wasn't anything to pay me back with,' she says bitterly. 'I met with his business partner to try and understand what was going on, and why they were haemorrhaging so much money. It turned out Simon had a gambling problem I didn't know about. He'd somehow managed to keep it hidden from me. He'd siphoned off the money I'd invested and used it on those online gambling apps, spending thousands. I split up with him right then – I was livid. The company they formed started bankruptcy proceedings the day after.'

'He would've paid you back eventually, wouldn't he?'

Even as I say the words, I know I'm wrong. I'm already viewing Simon through rose-tinted glasses and it's only two weeks since he died.

'I don't think so,' says Bec, echoing my own thoughts. 'Not that I'm going to see any of it now anyway.'

'What do you mean?'

'The idiot didn't leave a will. Under intestacy law, I'm not entitled to anything. Even my own money. It's gone. It's all gone.'

I rock back on the chair, stunned. 'I had no idea.'

'Me neither. We spoke about having wills done when we first got engaged. I had mine; I just hadn't updated it since we split up. I thought he had one, too. I thought …'

She drifts off, and turns her gaze to the garden beyond the window.

I clear my throat. 'How much did he owe you, Bec?'

'Eighty thousand pounds.'

Fucking hell.

'Is that why the police interviewed you when he died?' I say.

Her head snaps around. 'What do you mean?'

'I don't know.' I've gone too far; I can see that now. I should've kept my mouth shut. 'Sorry. I just wondered if they thought … you know …'

'If I killed him to get my money back?' She

sneers at me, anger flashing in her eyes. 'You can't talk. You had more motive than any of us to kill him. After all, if it wasn't for him dying you wouldn't be here. He was your final hope, remember?'

39

BEC

I HOPE IT WORKED.

I hoped it wouldn't come to this, but I'm resigned now.

Lisa will keep digging, keep asking questions, keep picking at the scab that's formed over the truth.

I have to protect her. I have to make sure she believes me.

I'm telling the truth about the money, at least. Simon really did coerce me into lending it to him.

I resisted at first, saying I didn't think it was such a good idea to do such a thing so early on in our relationship.

After that, he sulked.

He stopped suggesting nights out, saying he had

to work late to try and find a way to move the venture forward, that he was too tired for sex, that he was too stressed out wondering how they were going to seize the opportunity.

I became worn down, paranoid about spending my own money for fear of him judging me, that he might see a new pair of shoes as another nail in the coffin for the exciting opportunity he made me feel I denied him.

Of course, I gave in eventually. Three months of guilt was more than anyone should have to take and, in the end, I was too exhausted to argue anymore.

I went into my bank to transfer the money into his account, thinking the transaction was enough of a receipt.

I'm a fool, I know.

But I loved him once.

I tug at the bandages, impatient now to heal. The fire has turned to an aggravating itch and I can't wait to be rid of them. They are ugly, reminding me of what has happened and what I used to have.

I am angry with myself. I never thought I was the sort of person to give up like this, that I could be so desperate to finish it all.

I knew Lisa and Simon had been together for a while when they were at school studying their A-levels, and I don't know why they split up, but I never felt that I could talk to her about him until now.

Now that he's dead.

A few days ago, as I sat here, I wished that David hadn't saved me. I wish that he had let the blood flow out from me, let me sink under the surface of the bath water, and let me die.

Now, I feel a new determination. I want my life back.

Simon is gone. I don't have to answer to him anymore. No more arguments. No more worrying that he will snap at me, tell me I'm being stupid, tell me he knows better than me.

I realise I am clenching my jaw, and force myself to relax.

I'm going to have to find a new job, of course. Maybe even move away – it wouldn't be a bad thing to put some distance between me and the rest of them now.

Not after everything that has happened.

At least in a new town, perhaps a few hundred miles from here, I can start again. I can change my appearance, get a haircut, change the colour, and, if anyone asks me if I am that Rebecca Wallis who allegedly killed her boyfriend, I can laugh and tell them I don't know what the hell they're talking about.

Despite my bravado though, there is a dull ache where our friendship used to be. The five of us began fracturing apart from each other even before Simon died, and I don't think the ones who are left are going to stay in touch, to be honest.

I am scared, too.

What if the police decide they want to speak to me again? What if they take this as an admission of guilt, rather than an act of desperation to make it all end?

I push away the empty takeaway coffee cup and wonder if I should venture along the corridor and downstairs to the café for another one. I glance up at the wall, forgetting there are no clocks in this ward, and then decide to move to a different armchair across the room as a middle-aged man with stringy hair lowers himself into the one opposite mine and leers at me.

I need to get out of here. All this sitting around thinking isn't doing me any good. I never used to be like this. Simon shattered my confidence, as well as my bank balance and reputation.

When I finally told Mum and Dad what had happened, what he'd done to me, they were incredulous.

Surely not. Surely not Simon, not the future son-in-law they thought they were getting.

Even now, I'm not sure they believe me.

I haven't been allowed access to my mobile phone or a computer – something about ensuring I have a full recovery without being exposed to social media, I expect – but I told them where to find the paperwork, the evidence of what he had done.

I need them to know. I need them to know that I'm telling the truth about what he did.

Lisa, though. Lisa worries me.

Now that she has a new lease of life she seems determined to wreck everyone else's.

While she was ill, when things were so desperate, we all rallied around her, doing all we could to help. I hadn't realised at the time though how self-centred she had become – or was she like it before she got ill, but I hadn't noticed?

All I know now is that she really can't remember. I wish she would leave this alone, go back to work, do what she says she's going to do and get on with her life, and leave mine well alone.

She could do so much damage, and she doesn't even know it.

There's a flurry of activity near the door.

I suddenly wish I could stay in here, safe from the outside world, because the person standing in the doorway is the last person I want to see right now.

40

DAVID

I RUN a hand across my eyes and stare at the computer screen once more, battening down the panic that is threatening to rise.

Since Hayley stormed out of the café, I've alternated between wanting to phone her to apologise, and leaving her to stew.

I think she knows something, and I'm not ready yet.

I don't know if I will ever be ready.

Martin wanders past, whistling under his breath, oblivious to the turmoil of his employee's mind. He's been a good boss to me these past few weeks, giving me time off to visit Lisa, to mourn for Simon, to try to understand what my life's become.

At least he hasn't noticed my mistakes. I've been extra careful, double-checking – no, triple-checking – everything that I've worked on since I saw that first error. I can't afford to lose my job on top of everything else.

I lower my gaze to the computer screen again. The calculations are wrong. At this rate, the state-of-the-art roof will be lost with the first gust of wind that hits the client's house next winter. It's a beginner's mistake, and not the first one I have made this month.

I used to be good at this. I used to be able to block out the outside world and be lost within my work. It became a sanctuary, a way to escape. I could spend hours within the finite details of each design, turning someone's dream into a reality.

I enjoyed it, too and it's that abandonment that I'm trying to find again because it's my only release from what's going on around me.

Everything feels like it is unravelling, that I have lost control.

I realise with horror that in a situation like this, I'd turn to Simon for advice.

When I met him for the first time at university, I'd felt overshadowed by his personality. He was the one who people gravitated towards; there was something special about him, the way he could coerce anyone with a persuasive self-mocking charm. He used it on girls, he used it on the teaching staff.

He used it on all of us.

And yet, once he realised I wasn't a threat to his carefully constructed persona and that I simply wanted to walk in his shadow, he mellowed. I became trusted, a confidant, someone he could let into his inner circle without fear of being judged.

Needless to say, I used that to my advantage.

I knew everything about Simon.

I didn't necessarily want to know, but he couldn't help himself. Behind that nonchalant persona he carefully pieced together for the benefit of those he wanted to impress was a nervous, bitter, calculating man who used venom and spite to complain about those around him if they didn't pander to his every whim.

I became the firefighter; the one who poured cold water on the arguments he started, who made excuses for his behaviour, who lied on his behalf. All to earn his approval, his acceptance.

And look where that got me.

I glance around the office.

There are only six of us now, including Martin, after a whole swathe of European customers started fleeing for the Continent, no longer made to feel welcome on our shores and taking their multi-million property development funds with them.

A cost-saving exercise took place, as with so many other businesses. Thankfully, I had a hunch about what was to come and spent the weeks leading up to the redundancies ensuring my colleagues' work contained errors, that they took time off work with mysterious stomach cramps, or turned up late through some unfortunate circumstances such as flat car tyres.

It worked. I'm still here.

But, it's depressing. We used to have a laugh working here; now everyone sits with their heads bowed as if trying to make themselves as small as possible so they're not singled out when the next round of redundancies takes place.

The fear is crippling me.

Maybe I should run away like our customers did, set up a freelance business like Hayley has. Perhaps I could find work in Central or South America, put this last year behind me and pretend none of it ever happened.

Who am I kidding?

I am desperate to talk to Bec.

I need to know what she remembers.

She was always the most sensible one out of all of us, so to see her fall to pieces like this has been a shock. Out of all of us, she was the one who'd experienced the most recent loss, so I expected her to be the one to guide us if things got tough.

I didn't expect her to fall apart, to accept defeat so easily.

I clear my throat, check my mobile phone is in my pocket, and mutter something about popping out to grab coffees for everyone.

I'm running by the time I reach the stairs.

WHEN I TOLD Simon we'd be meeting at the Ragamuffin Bar before heading to the escape room, he'd sneered.

I had to concur – both of us preferred proper pubs that sold ale using brewing techniques centuries old, but the girls liked that sort of thing and expected something special for our last group outing.

Besides, we'd never been there before.

I've timed it right – the cocktail bar has only just opened and the place is quiet, with a lone bartender wiping down the granite bar as I push through the ornate oak-panelled front door.

I have to admit, the decor in here has been completed to a high specification. A rival architectural firm beat Martin to the contract for the shop fit, and the dark wooden flooring provides a striking contrast to the exposed brickwork of the old merchant store.

I glance sideways at the round table next to the window, six chairs arranged around it providing ample opportunity to people-watch the steady stream that crowds past during the lunchtime rush.

That's where we sat. Simon took the seat with his back to the toilets, insisting he needed to be able to see the bar, window and door at the same time. We'd all rolled our eyes and acquiesced, grumbling under our breath that, wherever we went, he got his way.

The mood had lifted with the first round of cocktails though, Lisa sticking with sparkling water but taking a sip from each of ours.

I swallow, and look away.

A mirror runs the length of the bar behind the

till, the shelves in front of it stacked with bottles of vodka, gin, whisky, vermouth and more spirits and mixers than I could ever name.

'Can I help you?'

The bartender pauses in his cleaning duties and rests both hands on the granite surface he's been polishing.

'I'm just checking the place out for my sister's birthday. It's her eighteenth. My parents want it to be somewhere they know she'll be safe.'

'We rarely get trouble here. It's not that sort of place,' he says, and then grins. 'We find the prices keep potential troublemakers away.'

I smile politely, and wonder how many times he's uttered those words.

'Besides,' he says, and points upwards, 'the whole place is covered by CCTV.'

'CCTV?' My mouth dries.

'Yes. You know – cameras. Any problems, it'll capture everything.' He returns to his polishing, and winks. 'Your sister will be perfectly safe here.'

I'm not listening. I've already turned around, hurrying towards the door, my sweaty palm leaving a streak across the brass plate fixed to the oak surface before I stumble out onto the street.

I inhale, gulping in exhaust fume-filled air to try to calm the panic that begins to seize me.

The Ragamuffin Bar has cameras. I hadn't even thought of that.

They would've seen us at our table that day.

What else did they see?

41

HAYLEY

THE AIR KISS is as fake as our cheery greetings, but it has to be done.

We haven't got a choice.

It's late morning, and it seems the other patients in this part of the hospital partake in a mass exodus towards the refreshments trolley I passed in the corridor and then rush to claim an armchair in here before their relatives arrive.

Bec is smiling when I turn back to her.

'Isn't there somewhere else we can talk?' I say. 'Somewhere more private?'

'No.'

Christ, she's enjoying this. I hitch my bag up my shoulder. 'How are you?'

'Better.'

She sounds it, too. This is the old Bec I remember. The savvy one, who had a personal pension, tax-efficient savings account and more, before any of us had even contemplated such things. The one who saved for holidays, shunned credit cards, and looked down her nose at the frivolous purchases I've shown her from time to time while citing special discounts at department stores.

Until she and Simon got together two years ago.

We all knew something was wrong, but none of us wanted to be the first to ask.

We were afraid of the truth.

Within six months of their engagement, I noticed a haunted expression in her eyes. She would jump with fright at the slightest unexpected noise – a door slamming, a raised voice, or when her mobile rang while the three of us were having coffee somewhere.

Lisa would roll her eyes, then watch as Bec would scuttle from our table, phone to her ear, her voice low and urgent.

'Summoned again,' she would say, her top lip curling.

I don't think I can ever forgive her now. She was the one who brought him into our circle of friends, after all.

When I later found out they had dated before university, I was livid.

'Why didn't you tell us?'

Lisa had shrugged. 'I didn't think it mattered.'

'You should have warned us.'

Yes, she should have.

Then we would've been able to protect ourselves, try to avoid him, try not to fall for his boyish charms and self-deprecating humour.

Instead, we became acolytes.

Lisa, too.

As I watch Bec's eyes narrow at the sight of the nurse entering the room and stopping to chat with each patient, I wonder why the hell Lisa never told us why she'd split up with Simon before starting university.

I should probably ask her again now that he's dead. Now that we have nothing to fear from him.

An enormous relief flooded through me that day as I stood staring at his prone body.

Afterwards, I realised I had been clenching my fists so hard, my fingernails had dug into my palms creating crescent-shaped cuts, a temporary reminder of the pain he had caused me.

And so, to Bec.

Because something is niggling at me. Something I have heard in passing.

Or did I imagine it? I'm not sure.

'Lisa was here earlier,' Bec says. 'In fact, you only missed her by five minutes.'

'Never mind.' I keep my tone light, try to hide the relief that I don't have to see her yet. 'So, when do you get out of here?'

'Tomorrow, with any luck.' Her smile falters. 'Back to reality.'

'Are you going straight back home?'

'God, no. I'm never going back there. My dad and brother have already been round there with a van and emptied the place. Sod the last few months' rent.'

'Where will you go?'

She snorts. 'Somewhere a long, long way from here.'

I swallow. There's no turning back now.

'Bec? Why did you do this? Why try to end it all?'

Her mouth forms a moue of regret, and then

she takes a deep shuddering breath. 'I'm not sure that I did.'

I frown, confused by her words. 'You sliced two four-inch scars down your arms, Bec. That seems to me that you wanted to die.'

Her face darkens, and her eyes narrow. A single tear rolls over her cheek, and her words are like acid. 'I should never have listened to you, you stupid bitch.'

Seconds later, I make my excuses and leave, bereft for a friendship that has been torn apart.

It was never meant to come to this.

My phone vibrates, and I pause to pull it from my bag, wondering if it's David, wondering if he's panicking by now.

My smile freezes, and I start to walk, faster this time as I re-read Lisa's text message.

WHAT DO U REMEMBER ABOUT GREG FISHER? L.

Shit.

With my head bowed and my eyes downcast, it's not until I'm almost back in the reception area that I hear a familiar voice and raise my head. I gasp, then side-step through lift doors that have almost closed, earning a reprimand from a hospital orderly with an empty wheelchair.

I don't care.

As the doors swish together, Detective Constable Angela Forbes stalks past me, and she's heading towards Bec's ward.

I don't go home straight away.

I'm shocked by Bec's words, by her admission that Simon coerced her into lending him money. I thought we were closer than that; that I was someone she could confide in but it seems I've been wrong.

I've been wrong about so many things.

I'm angered, too, by her insinuation that I had something to do with Simon's death.

She has no right to talk to me like that. It's not my fault he died and I got his kidney.

I leave the bus miles before the one at the end of Mum and Dad's street, deciding I need to walk the rest of the way.

If I arrive back at my parents' house with a

face like thunder, Mum's going to start asking questions that I don't have the answers to, and I don't need her analysing the argument I've just had.

As I wander across the road to the entrance to the Common, the cold November air prickles my flesh, and I tug down my coat sleeves to offset the sudden chill before finding a wooden bench that overlooks the lake.

The toddlers who are usually here with their parents are nowhere to be seen and I savour the mid-week calm as I watch a pair of ducks waddle across the grass.

A sense of unease clutches at my chest as my gaze lifts to the dark water beyond the birds.

The sight of the lake leaves a nauseating sickness in my stomach, and the fine hairs on my arms twitch in anticipation, forming goosebumps on my flesh.

I exhale, and lean back against the wooden slats of the bench.

I try to relax. I remind myself that I'm healthy, that I've been given a second chance, and that I have a life ahead of me. No matter how short a reprieve I've been given, I intend to do something with it.

With or without the others' help. I still haven't heard back from Hayley.

I shove my hands in my pockets and glare at the ducks that are now paddling towards the middle of the pond, their movements casting graceful bow lines across the water.

Despite telling David that I'm house-hunting here in Southampton, I wonder if staying in this area is wise.

Too many people know me now, thanks to that bloody journalist. Even if my boss can give me my job back, I don't know if I want it.

Bec's revelation about the money has left me repulsed.

I knew that Simon asked her for the loan.

I knew, because I was with him when he found out that the venture was going to need some capital to push it forward, to seize the opportunities he and his business partner had so carefully laid out in their plans.

Golden rays of light had shimmered through the net curtains of the loft apartment Simon rented next to the river. It cast soft tentacles across the carpet and over the cotton sheets that had crumpled beneath our lovemaking.

His mobile phone squawked an eighties film

soundtrack as it vibrated across the bedside table, rousing us from a sex-induced slumber.

Mollified by too many tequila shots the night before, I slipped out from under his arm as he answered the call and padded through to the bathroom, rummaging through the cupboards until I found some soluble painkillers and made my way out to the kitchen.

I knew I shouldn't have done it. I knew it was a mistake to go out for drinks with him while Bec was away. We'd been circling each other for weeks, laughing about old times, things we used to do when we dated. A chance encounter at a bar in town on the way home from work was all it took.

I filled two glasses with water from the tap, tipped a measure of the powdered solution into each and wandered back to the bedroom.

Simon was sitting up in bed, his dark hair dishevelled and his green eyes flashing with excitement.

He gulped the water, slammed the glass on the bedside table and then pulled me into the sheets with him, laughing.

'This is my chance, Lisa. I'm going to leave all the others in my wake, you bloody watch me. If I can borrow some money off Bec to get us started, I'll be rich in no time.'

I found out I was pregnant when I missed my period later that month.

We met at a pub on the other side of town, far away from where either of us lived, and nowhere Bec knew. Simon wanted to meet in a café close to his employers – by then he was trying to juggle two jobs at once without his boss finding out about the second one, the joint venture.

I wanted to meet somewhere public. I knew what his temper was like when he wasn't in control.

As it was, he sat staring at the table for a moment, silent.

His jaw clenched, and then he pushed his pint away. 'You'll have an abortion, of course.'

'Yes.'

I'd already decided that I would, but his statement still had the power to shock.

'And not around here, either,' he continued. 'Go private, not on the NHS. We don't want a record of it. You'll have to pay for it. All of my money's wrapped up in this venture now.'

I nodded, my throat raw.

'Lisa?'

I met his gaze, hopeful for some sort of apology

from him, or acknowledgement that I was frightened.

'If you ever tell Bec, I'll kill you.'

He pushed back his chair and left the pub.

I went up to Glasgow for the abortion. Told everyone it was a work weekend away. Team building.

Months later, I'd put my growing sickness down to the after-effects of the abortion. It was common, they said. You'll get over it, they said. You'll feel better in no time.

Then I received my diagnosis. I needed a kidney transplant, and soon.

It was retribution, I thought. The universe's way of punishing me for what I'd done.

I hug my arms around my stomach and close my eyes as another thought crosses my mind.

I'm glad he's dead.

43

DAVID

I LEAVE my bike chained within its rack in the car park under the office and instead take the bus across town to Hayley's place.

On the way, I hang on to the thought that we're friends, that she'll forgive me.

I use my sleeve to wipe the condensation from the window and peer out at a ragged sky, clouds tumbling over each other as a dark band of rain sweeps across the distant countryside, and then glance down at my mobile.

She won't answer her phone. After three rings, it goes through to voicemail. After leaving a message, I decide I'm not leaving any more. I need to speak to her in person.

And yes, I'll apologise.

I'll do anything to make this right, because we need each other right now.

There's no other way.

My thumb hovers over another name on the display.

Fuck it, I think, and hit the call button.

'West City Hospital Trust. How may I direct your call?'

'I'd like to be put through to the Carmichael Ward, please.'

'One moment.'

I glare at a teenager sitting picking his nose in the seat opposite mine. The bus slows for the next stop and I decide to walk the rest of the way. I'm nervous, cooped up like this and dependent on someone else's schedule.

I huddle under a shop awning as the old bus belches black and grey exhaust fumes before disappearing into the traffic, then press the phone closer to my ear as the call is connected.

'Carmichael Ward.'

'Hello, my name's David Marsh. I'm a friend of Rebecca Wallis.'

'Visiting times are over for today, I'm afraid, Mr Marsh.'

'Oh?' I'm thrown for a moment, and check my watch. 'But it's only—'

'I'm sorry, but that's the doctor's instructions.' She lowers her voice. 'Between you and me, she was exhausted after speaking with two visitors this morning, and then what with that police officer walking in here like she owned the place—'

I realise she's broken with protocol, and probably several hospital rules about privacy and patient confidentiality, but I don't care. The hairs on the back of my neck are standing on end, and I rest my other hand on the shop façade, my vision blurring.

'The police were there? Why?'

She makes a small noise in the back of her throat, evidently realising her error. 'Well, I'm sure it was just routine. You'll be able to come and see her tomorrow, from ten o'clock if that suits?'

No, that doesn't bloody suit.

I hang up, furious.

Evidently both Lisa and Hayley have been to see Bec, either alone or together, but neither of them have seen fit to tell me.

Me, the one who found her.

Me, the one who saved her life.

'Everything okay?'

The owner of the shop is hovering on the step, his brow furrowed.

I wonder if I've spoken out loud. I shake my head. 'I'm fine. Just going. Thanks.'

I turn on my heel and set a quick pace, putting as much distance between me and the shop as I can.

What the hell were the police doing speaking to Bec?

Hadn't they done enough damage? Why did they want to interview her again?

Didn't they believe her the first time?

I try Lisa next.

Lisa, easy-going Lisa will surely raise my spirits. She looked radiant by the time we left the pub the other day, chatting about her plans for the future and buying another house of her own. As I drove her back to her mum and dad's we spoke about what she could afford, and I was looking forward to joining her when she went out to choose furniture.

'You've got such an eye for detail,' she said. 'You architects are all the same. If you come with me, at least I know I'll end up with stuff that complements the house and doesn't clutter it.'

I'd driven home, high on her new vitality and energy. It's been so long since we've seen her like that.

But she isn't answering her phone, either.

The standard network message tells me she's either out of range or her phone is switched off.

There's a pub up ahead, and I decide I need a quick drink to calm my nerves. It's nothing fancy, just a hole in the wall establishment with a pool table on the left of the door as I push my way into the gloom and across to a bar that stinks of stale alcohol.

I order a scotch from the girl serving behind the bar, wrinkling my nose at her chewed fingernails as she hands me my change, and wander across to a corner seat next to the window. From here, I can peer out at the outside world and try to numb my churning mind.

I shouldn't have pushed my luck the other day. I shouldn't have taunted Hayley, but I couldn't help it. She was pissing me off, trying to second-guess what everyone else was thinking and I was tired of hearing it.

I dial her number again, and am both relieved and surprised that she answers.

She doesn't say anything though.

'It's me, David,' I say unnecessarily.

A silence drags out for what seems an age, and

then she speaks, but it's not the Hayley I know. She is cold, detached.

'What do you want?'

I take a deep breath. 'I wanted to apologise for yesterday. It was uncalled for. I don't know what came over me.'

The words come tumbling out; all the rehearsed lines forgotten.

A bitter laugh is choked back before she speaks again, and her words leave me terrified.

'Remember, I know what you did.'

44

HAYLEY

I HANG UP, cutting David off mid-sentence and try to shrug off the weariness that seeps into my muscles.

I don't want to have anything more to do with him.

The more I mull it over, the less I want to stay in touch with Bec or Lisa, either. At least then, they won't find out what Simon knew about me and maybe, hopefully, I can salvage something from all this. Before all the other stuff comes out.

I didn't mean to, you see. I couldn't stop myself.

When it first happened, we were in our final year at uni, and it was because I forgot.

I simply went into the department store in my lunch hour to kill some time rather than stay in the canteen and listen to the latest gossip about whichever celebrity was stuck on whatever island and likely shagging whoever.

Instead, I wandered around the displays of that season's dresses, dreaming of days out to far-flung places with a non-existent boyfriend and trying to calculate how many pay cheques from my meagre part-time job I'd need in order to afford one of the diamond-encrusted watches displayed under glass counters.

I don't remember picking up the lipstick.

I know I was considering buying a new shade before realising the time and that I'd have to get back for the afternoon lecture, but when I reached the end of the High Street and put my hand in my pocket after pressing the button for the crossing, that's what my fingers wrapped around.

I stood there, stunned for a moment before a loud *zap* reached my ears and the man next to me gave me a nudge.

'Come on, love, otherwise you'll miss it.'

My heart beat so hard at the interruption from my thoughts that I cried out in surprise. Luckily, he was already halfway across the road and didn't hear me, although the old woman beside me shot me a funny look.

I ignored her, hurried to the campus and took the stairs two at a time before locking myself in the ladies' toilet, sweat beading on my brow.

Once the fear subsided, a new sensation taunted me. One of bravado.

I'd got away with it, hadn't I?

None of the alarms had gone off. No one had come running after me.

And so it went on.

I could stop any time I wanted to, I told myself.

It's just a bit of fun.

No one gets hurt.

Until the night we were all at a distant acquaintance's wedding two years ago, invited out of politeness for attending the same classes at the university.

We'd been placed on different tables, but caught up at the bar in between courses of lavish food presented by a team of wait staff in tuxedos.

We huddled and giggled over glasses of vintage champagne at the extravagance, the drunken antics of the bride's mother, and the money being lavished on a wedding we were sure would end in divorce in under five years.

Then Simon had offered his arm and flashed

me one of his lopsided grins. 'Dance for old times'
sake?'

'Go on then.'

We sidled around the other couples, my hand in
his, his other resting on my waist, and spent the first
part of the song stumbling over each other's feet
until we found our rhythm. As I was relaxing into
the dance, he lowered his mouth to my ear and
said, very softly—

'Do you steal for the thrill, or because you
actually need to?'

'Pardon?'

Stunned by his words, I stopped so suddenly
that the couple next to us bumped into me.

Simon smiled and held up his hand to them,
then raised an imaginary glass to his lips and
winked.

They both laughed, took their places, and
danced away once more.

'I don't know what you're talking about,' I
managed as the closing bars of the pop tune
reached my ears.

'If you keep stealing things, you're going to get
caught.' He kissed my hand, never taking his eyes
off me as the music ended and the other dancers
applauded the band. 'Someone might report you.'

He dropped my hand then, and sauntered back towards the bar as if nothing had happened.

Even now, my mouth is dry recalling it all.

I tried, I really tried but within a few weeks I'd done it again.

I got home, my heart pounding, wondering if he'd seen me. Wondering if he was spying on me so that he could go to the police and tell them what I had done.

He must've spotted the new earrings, even though I'd waited weeks until I'd worn them – they were perfect for the summer party we all went to.

Two days later, a letter turned up. Not an email. Not a phone call.

A fucking letter.

And he wanted money, or else he'd write anonymously to my clients and tell them all about my secret shoplifting habit. It wouldn't matter how I tried to excuse any letters as the work of a spiteful individual, my business would be ruined so, of course, I paid him.

I couldn't stop shoplifting. I know, that sounds pathetic, but it was the thrill. I got away with it, for a while, and then six weeks ago another letter arrived.

I was terrified, and so when—

I emit a stifled cry as the doorbell trills.

I can't stop the gasp that escapes when I open the door.

Detective Constable Angela Forbes is on the doorstep, a steely glare aimed at me while behind her, two uniformed police officers hover at the garden gate.

'What do you want?' I manage.

'Hayley Matthews, you do not have to say anything...' She steps forward, reciting a string of words that I'm sure are second nature to her but confuse me as I move back, my hand going to my throat.

She can't be serious, surely?

'...anything you do say may be given in evidence.' A sly smile creases her lips and she holds out her hand. 'Come with me, please. We'll continue this conversation at the station.'

'I need to get my things.'

Forbes glances over her shoulder and beckons to the taller of the two uniformed officers, who then follows me through to the dining area and watches as I put my mobile in my bag and slip the strap over my shoulder.

Heat rises to my face as they wait on the garden path while I lock the front door and drop the keys into my bag next to my purse. I square my shoulders and turn in time to see the net curtain drop across the front bay window of number forty-seven across the street.

Forbes opens the back door of her car and watches dispassionately as I climb in. She slams it shut, and as she sits behind the wheel I hear the dull *thunk* of the internal locking mechanism click into place.

The uniformed officers drive off, lights blazing and, at first, I think they're going to lead us to the police station. However, at the end of the street they break off and head left, out to another call out I presume.

I realise that Forbes had them accompany her for the shock value, not because she saw me as a flight risk.

She wanted to embarrass me in front of my neighbours. She wanted to scare me into submission when I opened my front door.

And she wants me to tell her everything without a fight.

I clench my jaw and stare out the window as we pass through the centre of town, trying to ignore the fear that's now crawling through my veins.

Christ, fifteen minutes ago I thought I was the smartest woman I'd ever known. Now look at me.

I realise I'm shaking. I'm allowed a phone call, right? That's what they do on the television. I won't phone my dad – God, he'd be mortified and I'm sure as hell not trying to explain this to him. Lisa? Bec? And say what?

I turn back to face the front of the car and realise that by placing me behind the passenger seat, Forbes has ensured I can't watch her in the rear-view mirror. I can't make eye contact with her.

'I need the loo.'

'You can have a break at the station.'

She's an efficient driver, weaving through the traffic and not slowing down unless absolutely necessary. In half an hour, we slow opposite a six-storey concrete and glass building, and I realise this is it.

This is the police station.

Forbes steers the car around the side and towards the rear of a red-brick wall, adhering to the slow speed limit while my heart rate increases.

I can feel it in my neck.

This is the route by which all suspects are brought in for questioning. I've seen it on the news in the past, and murmur a silent thanks that there are no journalists with cameras hanging around.

This is just a misunderstanding, I tell myself. *I'll have this cleared up in no time.*

Forbes slings the car into a parking space parallel to the driveway and then leads me through two double doors at the side of the station.

It's noisy here; there is a thin man in his thirties yelling at the top of his voice, his body odour so overwhelming that I take a step sideways to try to avoid it. A uniformed police officer keeps one hand on the man's shoulder and talks to his colleague the other side of the desk. Her eyes are wide; she's only young and appears terrified of the tattooed and swearing individual the policeman has brought her.

'Through here.'

Forbes doesn't break her stride; she swipes her card across the panel to one side of a thick wooden door and gives me a gentle shove to get me away from the fracas now taking place at the custody desk.

I wonder if she brought me this way on purpose, to intimidate me. If she did, it's working. My legs are shaking as she pushes open a door to a room with a sign on it stating 'Interview Room One'.

'Sit.'

She gestures to a chair on one side of a table.

The pitted wooden surface is scarred and sticky, shining under the stark lighting. I keep my hands folded in my lap.

'Do you have a solicitor you wish to appoint, or do you wish one to be appointed on your behalf?'

I think of Mr Franchester, my dad's solicitor who helped him update his will two years ago. 'No, I don't have a solicitor.'

'We'll arrange a duty solicitor to represent you. Is there anyone you'd like me to call to advise them that you're here?'

I shake my head. 'No.'

To my dismay, Forbes leaves the room and shuts the door behind her.

I am left staring at the opposite wall, and wonder how the hell I'm going to survive this.

45

LISA

IT'S RAINING; a light, persistent drizzle that slowly soaks into my jeans by the time I walk out of the gates at the north end of the Common.

I stand at the kerb and pull the hood of my padded waterproof coat over my head, shoving my hands in my pockets.

I'm lost, cast adrift on a plethora of decisions that I can't make on my own. We always decided together. Where to go, what to do, who to socialise with.

Paralysis seizes me. I stand, frozen, as cars roar past, headlights seeking a way through the rain that is quickly turning torrential; brake lights flashing as drivers realise their error in following too closely to the car in front; the noise and clamour of a city in motion all around me.

I want to see it. I want to see the escape room again, but I'm struggling.

I curse my own stupidity for not bringing some painkillers with me in case I needed them. My recovery is progressing well, and I forget what I've put my body through, such is my relief that I've had a reprieve from death.

Despite my surgeon's best attempts, I am not superhuman after all.

I miss a bus by seconds, and squint through the mist that swirls across the pavement and up the road. It's not far, not really.

I can't make it, but I have to know.

I grimace as another bolt of pure fire stabs my abdomen and hope to hell I haven't caused any damage. Since moving the boxes in Mum and Dad's garage, my stomach muscles have twisted together, reminding me that I need to take it slow; I need time to heal.

Except I might not have time.

A car advances down the road towards me, a sign on its roof a welcome illumination.

I raise my hand as it approaches, the orange flash of an indicator blinking before it pulls to the kerb. It's covered in the livery of one of the local taxi firms, an extravagance I'd normally avoid.

But then, this is anything but normal.

Normal packed its bags and headed for the hills almost two weeks ago.

I wrench open the back door and collapse onto the seat behind the front passenger seat.

'A-Maze Escape Room.'

'No problem, love. Terrible weather to be out in.'

That saves me explaining myself to the driver, at least. The escape room is only a five-minute drive away from here, and on any other day – health permitting – I might have walked.

Not today.

I stare out the window, at figures dashing back and forth on the pavement as they try to get indoors, back to the office, back to work before getting too wet.

A woman struggles with a flimsy umbrella that has turned inside out, and then gives up and shoves it into a rubbish bin next to a bus stop, raises her bag over her head and begins to run. Her heels splash through puddles and rivulets of rainwater that rush towards the gutter, the drains bubbling over in shock from the deluge.

Thankfully, the taxi driver is silent save for the beat of his fingers against the steering wheel as a song on the radio plays out; an eye blink of a memory from my teenage years.

Humming to the song under my breath, I keep my face passive.

The driver adjusted his rear-view mirror after we set off, and I reckon it isn't angled at the lorry that grumbles along behind us.

I wonder if he saw the photograph of me that appeared in the newspaper. Maybe he's seen it online, but then I don't know what's happening on social media.

I don't go there.

Even when I checked my old timeline the other day, I didn't venture further past than seven years ago in case someone noticed. Because if one person noticed, someone else would, and my presence on the site would spread like a ripple across water.

Water.

I scrunch up my eyes as an image of the lake surfaces.

'Nearly there.'

The driver's voice jolts me to the present, and I stare wide-eyed between the front seats, gripping the passenger seat headrest so hard, my knuckles turn white.

Is this the right thing to do?

Should I be doing this?

The taxi slows to a crawl and I realise we're here, the driver craning his neck along a line of cars to our left, trying to find somewhere to pull over for a moment so he can collect his fare.

Fare.

I rummage in my purse, and glance at the meter on the dashboard. I want to use cash, not my card. I want to—

What?

Cover my tracks.

Don't leave a trace.

Stay anonymous.

All of that, and more.

I shove a ten pound note at the driver, tell him to round it up to eight quid, and shove the change in my purse before launching myself from the car.

Slamming the door, I hurry across to the doorway of a second-hand bookshop. The sign on the door says it's closed at the moment, which suits me.

I need a moment to just stand and think.

The taxi pulls into traffic, splashing through an

oil-slicked puddle and disappearing from sight. The pavement here is deserted. Away from the popular shops, away from the crowds.

I'm alone.

Peering up at the sky, I wrinkle my nose and try to work out if the rain is lighter, and then make my decision.

I need to look.

I leave the shelter of the bookshop doorway and turn left.

There were no parking spaces further up the road, so the taxi driver has left me a hundred metres or so from the escape room.

As I approach, I keep my eyes to the ground, wary of where I step; the cracked concrete pavers here are chipped and broken, slippery from dirt and grease that has mixed with the rain.

I don't want to stumble and fall.

Opposite, the Ragamuffin Bar is quiet, its Georgian exterior lit up with spotlights that entice people to stop, to come inside, relax. There are no people sitting at the tables in the windows, though.

I frown, trying to clutch at a memory that teases at the back of my mind, but it's gone before I get the chance to wrap my thoughts around it.

Turning my attention back to this side of the road, I stop.

There are boards across the front door of the A-Maze Escape Room. Two thick, wooden planks each the width of my hand have been nailed diagonally over the entrance.

A notice sealed in a plastic wallet has been fastened on the cross section.

I step closer, confused, until I read the words, and realise I'm not going to get the answers I'm seeking here.

CLOSED UNTIL FURTHER NOTICE.

It's been nearly twenty hours since I last saw DC Angela Forbes, so when she pushes open the door to the interview room and holds it open for my solicitor, I'm taken aback by the relief that courses through me.

It's quickly replaced by suspicion.

Where has she been?

Who has she spoken to?

What does she know?

She waits until my solicitor, Bernard Lamont, sits next to me, the chair scraping across the tiled floor setting my teeth on edge, and then nods to her younger colleague.

She waits until he hits the "record" button on

the machine next to us, then goes through the formalities. His name is Tom Darke, apparently.

Forbes opens a manila folder on the table in front of her and shoves a page towards Lamont. 'That's the formal authorisation you were seeking from the hospital. It appears your client's medical team agree that she's in a fit state to be questioned, so we'll recommence, shall we?'

She doesn't wait for him to respond. Instead she turns to me, her teeth bared in a crocodile smile.

'As we were saying when we last spoke, Rebecca. Where did you go after being interviewed here?'

I've already spoken to Lamont while Forbes wasn't around. I told him what I'm about to tell Forbes. I told him my suspicions, too, but he held up his hand.

'We might not need to go there,' he said.

Now I clasp my hands on the table in front of me. Another Lamont suggestion. Apparently, I'm too expressive.

'I went around to see Lisa,' I say. 'I hadn't seen her since her operation because I was here, talking to you.'

I keep eye contact with her, determined to make her see I'm telling the truth.

'How long were you there for?'

'About half an hour. Her mum let me in – she was going out shopping with a friend – and I left when she returned. So, yeah, about thirty minutes.'

Forbes leaned forward. 'What did you talk about?'

'Not much. Obviously, I was concerned for her health, and I wanted to know how the operation went. Lisa was upset that I hadn't visited her in hospital but then when I explained why I couldn't, she calmed down.'

'Was she angry?'

I shake my head. 'Frustrated, that's all.'

'And when you left? Where did you go then?'

'I drove home.'

'Did you go straight home?'

'Yes, of course I did. I needed a shower and I needed to rest. You'd kept me here for nearly twenty-four hours.'

Forbes leans back in her seat and raises an eyebrow at her colleague. 'You didn't shower and change before seeing Lisa?'

'Her house was on the way back to mine. I wanted to make sure she was all right.'

'You mean you wanted to find out what she remembered.'

I swallow. I'm not going to answer that.

'Detective, if you have a specific question you'd like to ask my client, then do,' says Lamont. 'But please don't make spurious statements.'

Forbes sneers at my solicitor and then turns her attention back to me. 'What did you do when you got home?'

'I told you.'

'Tell me again.'

I exhale, and let out some of the tension I've been bottling up. 'When I opened the back door—'

'The back door?'

'I didn't want my neighbour to see me, all right? I didn't want her asking me questions, or spreading rumours to the other neighbours. She gossips.'

'That would be… Mrs Dawson?' Forbes checks her notes.

'Yes.'

'Go on.'

'So, I cut through the alley at the back and came in that way. Like I said, the kitchen stank – the bins needed to be emptied. I cleaned up, and then tried to watch some TV before I went to bed. I couldn't sleep, so I came downstairs and played games on my phone for a bit. Before I knew it, it was morning. I was still a bit woozy – I drank too much wine during the night, I think, so I decided to have a soak in the bath.'

'And you took a kitchen knife with you?'

I lower my gaze to the table and rub my thumb over a cut in the wooden surface.

Did I?

'I don't remember.'

'Tell me what you do remember.'

'I filled the bath, and while I was doing that I thought it'd be a good idea to listen to some music as well. To calm me down.'

'Did you lock the back door?'

'What?'

She rests her arms on the table and leans towards me. 'Did you lock the back door before you went upstairs?'

I frown. 'Yes. Yes, I did. I always do if I'm going to spend any time upstairs.'

'Okay. So, you've got your bath running and your music playing. What happened next?'

'I – I got in the bath, I suppose.'

'What were you listening to?'

'Just a random playlist. Favourite tracks, that sort of thing.'

'Did the water get cold?'

'I—'

I don't remember.

I don't remember letting the water get cold. I remember topping it up and sloshing the water around so the bubbles would form again without having to put more of the bath soak in, the scent of berries filling the room as the mirror steamed up.

'How long were you in the bath before you decided to cut your wrists open?'

Forbes hasn't waited for my answer to her last question, so this next one takes me aback.

I'm not ready for it, not prepared. I close my eyes and try to focus.

I don't remember deciding to end it all.

What I do remember is vowing never to drink Pinot Noir again, and I remember going upstairs to run a bath so I could relax and mull over my options.

I remember the sensation of a breeze on my neck as I lay back in the bath, and wondering if I'd left a window open somewhere.

Because I'd definitely, absolutely, locked the back door.

My eyelids fly open.

Hadn't I?

47

LISA

How DID we get to this?

We were close-knit once. Thick as thieves, people said at university. We had dreams, plans for the future.

Bec's words stung me, hit me hard. Now I want to talk to her again, to find out why she felt the need to lash out like that.

All of us, the ones who are left, are circling each other like opposing magnets. We get close, but not close enough to let down our defences.

Why not?

I press the entry for Hayley's mobile number, but it goes to voicemail again. Why is she ignoring me?

Has she argued with Bec as well?

I need to speak to both of them, and soon. Finally, the effects of the general anaesthetic have left my system and the fog that has clouded my thoughts since the transplant operation has lifted, but there's something else.

Something blocking my memory of that afternoon in the escape room.

I don't leave another message for Hayley. If she doesn't want to talk to me then there's not a lot I can do about it until she comes to her senses.

A flash of movement outside the front window catches my eye, and my heartrate ratchets up a notch. Has that journalist found out where I live?

I'm on my own, and not sure I can cope with another barrage of questions.

The doorbell rings, and I take a breath before moving from the living room to the hallway. If it is the journalist, then I'm going to give him a piece of my mind. I'm going to—

David is standing on the doorstep, his hair dishevelled and his phone in his hand.

'Oh, it's you.'

'Everything all right?' he asks.

'I suppose so.'

'Are your mum and dad out?'

'Yes.'

'What is it this time? Let me guess – another cinema trip, right? Period drama?'

'Ha ha. No, some sort of biopic about a rock band.'

'Well, well, well. I'd have never have thought it of them. Can I come in?'

'Sure.'

I step to one side and slam the door after him, the frosted glass shuddering from the impact.

'You seem tense.' He's frowning, his head cocked to one side. 'Everything okay?'

I wrap my arms around myself. 'I thought you might've been that journalist. The one who was at the hospital.'

'Has he been pestering you since?'

'No.' I force a smile. 'I'm just being paranoid. Have you been to see Bec?'

He frowns. 'No. Apparently, I missed visiting hours. I didn't know they were letting anyone in yet.'

'Yes, only yesterday. I just happened to be over there having some more tests when I bumped into her parents. They told me the nursing staff were happy with her recovery, so I went in.'

'Why hasn't Bec phoned me?'

I put my hands up to placate him. 'Hey, it's

probably nothing to worry about. I'd imagine she's still exhausted from everything.'

'Her parents could've called me. After all, it was me who saved her.'

'Well, I don't know. I've been trying to phone Hayley and Bec today and neither of them are answering. Just keep trying. I'm sure you'll get through eventually.'

He's pacing the carpet now, his face downcast and his eyes roaming the gold flecked pattern amongst the russet yarn. He seems on edge, angry.

'Did you want to see me about something? It's just that I was going to make some phone calls to see if I could start viewing some houses later in the week.'

I'm lying through my teeth, but his demeanour is making me nervous, and I don't know why. I move to the front door and reach out for the handle.

I don't make it.

His hand shoots out and slaps mine away, and I cry out with shock.

'Wha—'

'Don't do that.'

He shoves me aside, and stands with his fists

clenched at his side, his eyes flicking to the living room and back.

It's like he's half here, half not. As if he's—

'Your transplant. It was meant to save your life.'

I frown. 'It did.'

'But you told me you might only live for another ten years.'

'David, what's going on?'

'You were meant to live. For a long time.' He rubs his hand across his jaw, then mutters under his breath and peers through the frosted glass in the door.

'What did you say?' I take a step closer, narrowing my eyes.

His gaze snaps back to me. 'I said, it changes everything.'

'Like what?'

'My plan. My plan for us.'

'Us?' I choke out a laugh, heat rising in my cheeks. 'David, there is no *us*. Where on earth did you get that impression from?'

He bares his teeth at me, and I side-step, holding up my hands. He moves closer, and I whimper.

His brown eyes are piercing, boring into me. I wonder how I never realised how much evil was in the depth of that gaze, before a new realisation hits me.

'You killed him. You killed Simon, didn't you?'

He shakes his head. 'No, that's not true. Not really.'

'But you've just said it yourself. You—' I stumble backwards, my heel catching the bottom stair tread. I land on my backside, jarring my spine but I'm numb, blood rushing in my ears. I can't process what he's said. 'Why?'

I don't recognise the voice; it's high-pitched, hysterical, terrified.

Mine.

He moves then, too fast for me to react, and drags me onto the floor, straddling his legs either side of my body, running his eyes over me.

I yelp as his thigh knocks against my wound, but he doesn't react to my cry of pain. I try to wiggle free, to loosen my wrists from his grip so I can attack his face, but I don't have the strength.

Instead, his eyes are dead, his gaze boring into me and I realise I'm fighting for my life.

'Why?' I say, choking out the words.

'You should have left it alone, Lisa,' he says, his voice dull. 'That was what we all agreed.'

48

DAVID

IN AN INSTANT, I'm back there, back at the lake, back at university that first winter.

I let Simon think it was his idea, of course. A suggestion here and there in the days leading up to it.

That despite his slight build, Greg was stronger, faster. That Greg could probably beat him.

That Greg had told me he could.

I chipped away, bit by bit, until finally—

'Let's have a race.'

We were in a pub across the road from the Common, debating what to do during the half-term break. Out of ideas and bored, we weren't yet ready to call it a night, but getting close.

Simon slammed his empty pint glass onto the

chipped varnish of the table and belched. He looked at each of us in turn.

Bec frowned. 'A race?'

'Not you, of course.' Simon pointed to Greg, then me. 'Just the boys.'

'What sort of race?' said Greg.

The smile that formed at the corner of Simon's mouth didn't reach his eyes.

'A special race.' He pushed his glass out of the way and leaned his arms on the table, not noticing the pools of condensation leaching into his pale-grey sweatshirt. 'Two circuits of the lake. Tonight. Bet you can't do it.'

Bec twisted in her seat and peered through the window. A Unibus drove past, its headlights picking out the fine snow that had started falling as we made our way to the pub a couple of hours before.

'You'll freeze,' she said.

'Not if we keep moving,' I said.

Simon reached over and shook my shoulder. 'See, even you're tempted.'

I smiled. 'I'd beat you.'

'Oh – fighting talk.'

The others laughed, but I noticed Greg didn't join in.

'What do you reckon, Fisher?' said Simon. 'Think you can beat me?'

'I reckon he could,' said Lisa. She leaned into him, nudging him gently with her elbow.

Greg smiled down at her and winked.

I clenched my fists under the table, out of sight and forced myself to relax my jaw.

'You're crazy,' said Bec, and shivered. 'Look at it out there.'

'I'll do it,' said Hayley.

'It's boys only,' said Simon.

'Scared I'll beat you?' She jutted her chin out.

She's drunk, and unaware of how loud she is.

'You can join in, if you want,' I say, in an attempt to mollify her.

'Awesome,' said Hayley. She twisted her glass of vodka and tonic in figures of eight on the table, leaving a trail of condensation. 'We'd have to be careful. If we get caught, the university might kick us all out. They have rules about this sort of thing.'

'So, we don't invite anyone else,' said Simon. He peered past Greg towards the bar.

A group from the business school were spread around two tables under the television, their attention taken by a highlights programme of an

Ashes test match being played in Adelaide, and no one was looking at us.

The rest of the pub patrons were locals, each engrossed in their own conversations.

Simon turned back to us. 'Perfect timing. Bec's right – no one's going to be walking around now, are they?'

'Why?' said Lisa.

'What?' Simon's head snapped around.

'Why a swimming race? Why now?'

Simon pointed at Greg. 'Because I reckon I can beat him. David reckons I can't. We have to settle this once and for all. Are you a man or a boy, Fisher?'

I saw it, then. The defiance in Greg's eyes.

His brow puckered, and then he reached forward, picked up his pint of Guinness and drained it.

'We should have a shot of whisky,' he said, his broad Glaswegian dialect exaggerated by the alcohol. 'My grandpa always swore by it, to keep the chill away.'

'I'll get them,' said Hayley.

I watched as she wove between the tables, a few heads turning as she passed. I wondered what any of them saw in her. Her eagerness to please would work to my advantage though – good looks were a poor substitution for loneliness; her desperation to fit in was her own worst enemy.

She returned five minutes later with a tray and six glasses. An amber liquid splashed at the bottom of each.

Bec raised an eyebrow as she took hers. 'Doubles?'

Hayley grinned as she slid the tray onto an empty table next to ours. 'I figured we'd need it.'

Six glasses clinked together as we toasted Simon's challenge.

I closed my eyes and winced at the burn of the spirit as it slid down my throat, thinking it was so typical of Hayley to buy the cheap stuff.

Moments later, we shrugged on coats, wrapped scarves around our necks and tumbled out of the door into the street.

The darkened entrance gates to the Common loomed opposite.

'Not going to chicken out on me now, are you?' said Simon.

'Not a chance in hell, you southern softy,' said Greg.

We laughed as we ran across the road, a car splashing past us in our wake.

Snowflakes splattered across my cheeks and nose as we followed the curve of the dirt and gravel path amongst the trees, moving further away from civilisation and closer to the dark waters of the lake.

The reed beds and trees gave the place a sense of calm and tranquillity in the warmer months, but now, as the narrow path opened out to a grass expanse and split into two, the lake seemed foreboding. It was only a few metres deep, but plunging into it in these temperatures would be deadly.

The island in the middle seemed to beckon us closer, and our pace slowed as we drew near.

'Whoa!'

Bec cried out as she stumbled at the water's edge, and then slapped Simon's arm. 'You idiot – I could have fallen in.'

He grinned, and then pulled her into a drunken hug. 'I'd have saved you.'

'You're still an idiot.'

Greg moved away, and peered into the darkness. 'All right, how do you want to do this?'

Simon pointed towards the copse of trees to our right. 'That's our starting point. The land slips down to the water, so it'll be easier getting in and out.'

He led the way, humming under his breath.

I hung back, my hands shoved deep into my pockets, and wondered if I had the stamina for what was to come.

I had to.

There was no other way.

By the time I had reached the beach Simon had described, I was a few paces behind the others and sweating.

I tugged my scarf away from my neck and loosened the zip of my thick jumper, letting the cold air whisk the heat away.

Greg and Simon stood at the edge, water lapping at their boots while Hayley hovered a few steps to their right.

'What do you reckon?' said Simon as I joined them. 'Two circuits around the lake, keeping to the deep water around the island, then back here.'

Greg said nothing. He kicked at a stone, the soft *plop* as it hit the water the only sound.

'This is silly. You don't have to do this.'

I turned at Lisa's voice.

She stood, arms hugging her side, her breath fogging on the air. Her hair spiked out from under her woollen hat, and at that moment I thought she was the most beautiful being in the world.

'She's right,' said Bec.

She huddled next to Lisa under the trees, waiting for an answer.

'What do you think?' Simon hadn't turned away from the lake. 'Race, or quit?'

I shivered.

'Race,' said Hayley, her words slurring a little.

'Race,' said Greg, and began to pull off his boots.

We didn't hang about after that. As we stripped down to our boxer shorts, and Hayley peeled off layers to reveal a matching black bra and knicker set, the perilous weather conditions became more and more apparent. A freezing blast of air moved across the lake's surface and whipped our bare skin.

We all swore – profanities that let out the shock, but not the fear.

Not for me.

Greg and Simon seemed high on adrenalin, laughing and joking as they hopped up and down, waiting for me.

Hayley was being her normal self – desperate to fit in, to be accepted.

'For fuck's sake, David, get a bloody move on,' said Simon.

Finally, we were all ready. We lined up on the

shoreline, and Greg glanced over his shoulder to where Lisa stood.

'Count us in, babe.'

'You're all crazy.' She sighed, but joined us at the edge. 'Three, two, one—'

I ran into the shallow water, my bare feet sinking into silt and stones. Mud oozed between my toes.

'Shit.'

Hayley let out a shriek as the icy water slapped against her skin, but she kept going.

We stumbled into deeper water, cursing the sharp stones and whatever else was down there that tried to thwart our progress, until a buoyancy claimed me, and I began to strike out, keeping my focus on the street light bobbing through the trees.

We swam side by side; Simon on the far left, Greg and Hayley in the middle, then me.

I recalled my own advice – *keep moving. Don't let your body register the cold*, I reminded myself. There was a long way to go yet.

And there was. I'd never appreciated the girth of the lake when I'd shot past on my bike over the previous months but then, swimming in its cold depths, my insignificance tightened my chest.

I risked a glance to my left.

Hayley powered through the water, keeping behind Simon.

Greg's strokes were methodical, determined, but he had none of their speed.

That was fine by me.

As Simon and Hayley pulled forward, I moved across to take their place, keeping pace with Greg but giving him a little headway.

We circled the lake once, and I looked at the shoreline to see Lisa and Bec at the water's edge, their pale faces staring back at us.

I turned my focus back to our progress as we turned away from them and began to circle behind the island once more.

'Fuck.'

I blinked. Simon was pulling forward to easily take the lead.

Beside me, Greg cursed again then slowed.

'What's wrong?' I gasped.

'Cramp.'

Perfect.

I knew he didn't use the gym like Simon did, and I knew my clandestine swimming practice would give me an edge.

'What's wrong?' Hayley had stopped, treading water as she peered back through the gloom at us.

'What is it?'

'Keep going,' I urged. 'He's just got cramp. We'll catch you up – don't let Simon win.'

She raised her hand in reply, then took off after him, her arms powering her through the water.

The splashes of their progress receded around the final bend of our makeshift race circuit, leaving Greg and me in the shadows.

Alone.

He groaned through his teeth, and then stopped, treading water.

'Keep moving,' I said. 'It's too cold to stop.'

'I can't.' His silhouette bobbed in front of me as I circled him, a slow breast stroke that enabled me to keep my muscles from seizing up in shock.

The lake was only three metres deep here, but it didn't matter in these temperatures. If he stopped swimming, he'd be in trouble.

He cried out then, a moment before his mouth and nose went under and he resurfaced, spluttering.

I kept quiet, watching, waiting until his movements spun him around, his back to me.

Then I surged forward, placed my hands on his shoulders and forced him under.

He squirmed, his bones and sinews fighting against my grip. Bubbles rose to the surface; a sure sign I was winning, that soon his body would go limp, give up its fight.

Die.

I said the word under my breath as he stopped struggling.

I didn't let go. I counted to twenty, and then turned and powered back towards the beach under the trees, strong strokes that left me gasping, exhilarated.

Ahead, I could see four figures jumping up and down, the cries of excitement carrying over the water, cheering me on.

I smiled as I hauled myself out of the lake.

Because even though Simon had come first, I knew it was me who'd won the race.

49

LISA

David gives a slight shake of his head, and focuses his gaze back to me, his lip curling into a snarl.

His hands move from my wrists to my neck, and he begins to squeeze.

I wriggle under his weight, trying to ignore the pain that cleaves my torso and stomach. I prise my fingers under his, desperate to find a way to loosen his grip around my throat.

He's crushing my windpipe, and I can't breathe. I can't suck a single breath into my desperate lungs.

A fresh terror sweeps through me as I realise I'm going to pass out.

And that if I pass out, I will die.

I grit my teeth, then slap at his face with my

open palms, forcing the heel of my hand to smash against his nose, his ears, his lips. Anything soft that I can damage.

Blood bursts from his nose, arcing across my face, and I screw up my eyes.

His weight shifts, and his grip loosens for a moment.

I open my eyes.

David gasps, arches his back and cranes his neck back so I can't reach his face anymore.

He grins through the blood pouring from his nose, a grotesque, manic expression in his eyes.

Then his hands wrap around my throat again.

'Go on,' he says. 'Fight. You won't win.'

His head whips around as someone starts ringing the doorbell.

'Tell them to go away, Lisa.'

'Help me!'

The backhanded slap comes from nowhere, the sound reverberating off the wall next to me, the pain from his knuckles against my cheek excruciating.

I'm weakening, losing consciousness, and I'm beginning to wonder if I imagined another voice.

Then, through the roaring of my own heartbeat

in my ears, I can hear someone banging on the door, and a familiar voice calls through the letterbox.

'Lisa?'

The banging grows louder, interspersed with shouted orders but David doesn't seem to notice.

He's mesmerised, tangling his hands in my hair before he lowers his face to mine.

My lips quiver as a solitary tear rolls down my cheek.

He strokes my face, running his hands down my ribcage, his fingers tracing the bones underneath the thin skin, and then he pauses, hovering over my bruised abdomen.

'I wanted you. I did it all for you, Lisa.'

A crashing, splintering noise reaches me, and I cry out with relief.

David is dragged away from me, yelling as he's restrained.

I let out a shuddering, gasping breath and try to sit up, but there's a hand on my shoulder, a calm voice slicing through the panic.

'It's okay, Lisa. Deep breaths. Sit there for a moment.'

I do as I'm told, and watch as two uniformed

officers haul David to his feet. They're none too gentle about it.

He sneers at me, as if he's going to spit at me or something but they spin him around and march him past the broken door, heading outside. I can hear the squawk of a radio and one of them talking to him in a low voice, telling him that anything he does say could be used in evidence.

Evidence?

I lower my gaze to my abdomen and lift my sweatshirt. The remnant stitches are fine, the bruising is not. I cry out as I lower my top, my fingers brushing against my wound.

'Here. Stand up.'

I twist around and look up, and I can't stop the sharp intake of breath, wondering why I didn't recognise the voice.

It's DC Angela Forbes, and she actually looks concerned.

I say nothing, but take the proffered hand and haul myself to my feet, then bend over and rest my hands on my knees as the room spins.

'Take it easy,' she says.

'I haven't got a lot of choice.' I blink, and try to focus. 'How did you know? Why did you come here?'

When she doesn't answer, I straighten and turn to face her.

Her lips are pursed, and then she utters words that send a chill to my core.

'Lisa Ashton, you do not have to say anything …'

50

LISA

I straighten my shoulders as Forbes enters the room but I'm surprised to see the man behind her.

Mortlock, the detective who came to Mum and Dad's house last weekend, sits opposite the solicitor who's been appointed for me.

Forbes drags out the chair opposite mine, slaps a manila folder on the table between us and then gestures to her superior.

He reaches out, starts the recording machine at the far end of the table and recites the formalities, his voice clear and unwavering.

Amongst these people, in their business suits and shirt sleeves, I'm scruffy in my creased sweatshirt and old jeans. I wish I could've put on some clean clothes, some make-up, at least had the chance to run a brush through my hair. I understand now why Hayley is always so immaculately dressed.

It's her armour.

I swallow, try to ignore the lump in my throat and wonder why I'm here.

I was the one who was attacked, so why am I being treated like a suspect? Don't they have rules for victims of assault? Shouldn't I be somewhere else, being looked after?

'Are you okay, Lisa?'

Forbes's opening question throws me for a moment. I stutter a response before I clear my throat and try again.

'Yes.'

Because I am, I realise. They have David under arrest, don't they? He can't hurt me now. 'How did you know?'

The question is out before I can stop it, and Forbes holds up a hand.

'We'll get to that. When did you first hear that Rebecca Wallis had tried to take her own life?'

'After the ambulance left her house. David sent me a text message.'

'Can you confirm this is the message that you were sent?'

She slides across a sheet of paper, and I read the transcript that must have been taken from David's phone.

I sigh, and force myself to concentrate. I have no idea what this has to do with David attacking me, but if Forbes wants to drag this out to impress her boss, then so be it.

'That's it, yes.'

'What happened next?'

'I wanted to go to the hospital, to be there for Bec. I can't drive at the moment, not after my transplant operation, so Mum took me there.'

'What happened when you got to the hospital?'

'Hayley and David were waiting. Hayley said Bec tried to kill herself. She said there was blood everywhere.'

'Had she been inside the house?'

'I don't think so, no.'

'So how did she know there was blood everywhere?'

'I don't know. I suppose David told her.'

'Who else was at the hospital?'

I cross my arms over my chest. 'That bloody journalist. The one who wrote the story about Bec supposedly killing Simon.'

'What did he say?'

'I can't remember. Something about how did I feel about her trying to kill herself. David—'

I break off at the memory. David had come to my rescue. David had told the journalist to get lost, and had grabbed the man by the collar before walking him to the door. He'd protected me from the reporter.

So, why did he just attack me?

'Lisa?'

I look up, to see Forbes and her boss watching me.

'What?'

'What did David do?'

I tell her. 'I've never seen him like that before. He was never aggressive.'

'Not in all the time you've known him?'

'No.'

'Do you have any idea why Rebecca tried to kill herself?'

'I assumed it was because that news story was published about her. About you lot holding her for questioning. After all, you made it look like she'd killed her ex, didn't you? Did you leak that story? Did you speak to that reporter and tell him what you thought she'd done? It's your fault she nearly died, isn't it?'

My voice is rising, but I can't help it. I'm furious now that I've realised what Forbes must've done, just because she didn't have any evidence and couldn't charge Bec.

The solicitor, an elderly man, reaches out and places his hand on my forearm. I glance across to him, and he shakes his head, his blue eyes piercing.

'I can assure you we didn't speak to the press,' says Forbes. 'We have strict protocols in place for how and when we engage with the media, and neither I nor anyone else on this investigating team contacted—' she glances down at her notes '—Scott Nash or Stella Barrett. However, we've interviewed Mr Nash in the past half hour and it transpires that he did receive a tip-off.'

'From who?'

'David Marsh.'

She may as well have punched me in the stomach. The breath leaves me in a drawn-out gasp, and I place a hand on the table to steady myself.

'Why?'

'We were hoping you could tell us.'

I can't think straight. Why would David do that? 'I don't know.'

'Well, let me put a theory to you,' says Forbes. She shuffles in her seat, clasps her hands together on top of the folder. 'It's our belief that David thought Rebecca knew something. Something that could harm him. Knowing the delicate frame of mind she was in from both losing money to her ex, Simon Granger, Granger's death, and being held for questioning here, he decided to tip the balance in his favour. He leaked the story to the journalist knowing it'd probably cause Rebecca harm, and everyone else would believe that she'd try to take her own life.'

My throat is dry as I listen, my insides twisting as her words sink in.

'Then,' she says, 'David enters her house – he knows where the spare key to the back door is hidden – and hears her in the bath. While he's taking a knife from the block in the kitchen, he notices that Rebecca has been looking at old photographs from when you were all at university. What does the name Greg Fisher mean to you?'

I gasp, but I can't get the words past my lips. How does she know about Greg? Has Bec told her? Did Hayley break her silence?

Forbes shrugs at my silence, then continues. 'While she is relaxing in the bath listening to music, David enters the room and holds her underwater until she stops breathing. Then he uses the kitchen knife to slice open her wrists. Afterwards, he runs back outside, hollering for the neighbours to help him, and calls triple nine. By the time the ambulance turns up, he's hauled her out of the bath and is pretending to attempt CPR.'

'But she lived.'

'She's a very lucky woman, according to the paramedics,' says Forbes. 'They were only two minutes away when the call came through, on their way back to their base. She was seconds away from dying.'

'But you have to charge him, right?' I spin around to face the solicitor. 'They have to charge him, yes? I mean, he's attacked me, tried to kill Bec—'

I turn back to Forbes as a thought punctures through my tirade. 'Did he kill Simon, too? Is that why we're here?'

She watches me, her gaze unwavering, and then—

'It's not as simple as that, is it, Lisa?'

51

LISA

I COULD HEAR David's teeth chattering as he emerged from the water.

Hayley ran towards him with his clothes, and he used his scarf to towel off the worst before pulling his sweatshirt over his head.

He had one leg in his jeans when he turned back to the lake.

'Where's Greg?'

Our excited chatter froze.

'He was in front of you, wasn't he?' Simon shoved his boots on his feet but didn't lace them up. He moved to the edge of the grass and peered into the darkness.

'He stopped swimming on the other side of the island,' said Hayley, her brow furrowed.

'He slowed down. Said he had cramp.' David's voice notched higher as he paced back and forth. 'I stayed with him and we trod water for a bit, but then he said he was all right, so we struck out.'

'Maybe he's cramped up again,' said Bec. She linked her arm through mine, and kept her voice upbeat. 'Come on, Greg!'

I couldn't swallow. My tongue stuck to the roof of my mouth, and I gagged.

'Greg,' I managed. 'Where are you?'

Hayley began to cry softly, until Simon turned to her and told her to shut up.

'I'm trying to listen,' he said.

We drifted apart, fanning out along the side of the lake, and I tried to squint through the darkness.

'Greg?'

I could hear the echo of my voice across the water, and clamped my mouth shut.

I sounded scared.

'Maybe he reached the island,' said Bec as we met back at the same spot where the boys and Hayley had entered the water. 'Maybe he's stranded there.'

'Greg!' Simon cupped his hands around his mouth and yelled. 'You there?'

We were still standing under the trees ten minutes later.

By then, I was crying.

'What do we do?' said David. 'Should we tell someone?'

'And get kicked out of university after we've just started? No, thanks.' Simon stood at the shoreline, his eyes wide. 'We can't. I need to graduate. We all do, right?'

David leaned over, tied his bootlaces, and then straightened and turned to us. 'Okay, this is what we have to do. This never happened. This never gets spoken of again.'

'What?'

'We can't!'

I looked at Bec and Hayley, saw the shock in their eyes, and turned to David.

'I can't believe you said that. We need to do something.' I pulled out my mobile phone. 'Fuck, there's no signal here.'

'The pub will still be open,' said Bec. 'We can raise the alarm and get someone to call the police.'

'Wait – David's right,' said Simon. 'If we do that, we're finished. Greg agreed to it. It's not like it's our fault. If they find his body, we say we argued with him after leaving the pub and he walked off in a temper. We don't know where he went.'

'We have to all stick to the story, no matter what questions we get asked,' said David, nodding. 'What happened here was an accident. It's not our fault.'

Hayley staggered, her hand to her mouth. 'They can't blame us for this, can they?'

'They might,' he said. 'How do you think it would look? He knew the dangers.'

I stood, stunned, as Simon began to walk away, and then one by one we drifted after him, David and me bringing up the rear.

David placed his arm around my shoulders and kissed the top of my head. I could smell the lake on him; a rotten, stagnant sweetness. He scowled at me when I pulled away, and I held up my hands to ward off his harsh words.

He shook his head, then shrugged. 'I'm sorry, Lisa. I tried to help him.'

In the days and weeks that followed, we closed ranks.

Shock turned to guilt, guilt turned to a quiet terror.

Terror that someone would find out what happened. Terror that something so stupid had turned to tragedy.

Terror that Greg's body would float to the surface.

But it never did.

It's why none of us moved away. We daren't. We had to be sure.

We would take turns to visit the lake, every few weeks. Walk the perimeter, peer into the reeds, pray that he would stay down there, lost forever.

After the police filled the Common with patrol cars and sniffer dogs, after we'd held our breath while divers searched the three lakes in the park, after his parents made an impassioned plea for information from their home in Glasgow for their son to contact them, and after they made a special trip south to visit the university to meet his fellow students, it fell silent.

The lake kept its secret. They never found his body.

And, once a year, on that same date, we would congregate under the trees and silently raise a glass of whisky to him, and hope we never, ever saw his face again.

Except in our nightmares.

None of us could prevent that.

52

LISA

I SHAKE MY HEAD, force myself to focus on the present.

'What does this have to do with—'

I pause mid-sentence, my jaw slack, and then turn to the solicitor beside me.

He says nothing, merely jots a note on the A4-sized notepad in front of him, and clears his throat.

I turn back to Forbes, my eyes wide. 'What's going on?'

'David tried to kill Rebecca because he was afraid that she was going to come back to us and tell us the truth,' says Forbes. 'The truth about what happened to Simon Granger. The truth about what happened to Greg Fisher.'

Next to her, Mortlock shifts in his seat but says nothing.

Forbes pushes her chair back and walks to the door, opens it and takes a laptop that a younger detective in a suit hands to her. She nods her thanks and comes back to the table. She flips open the laptop and turns it around to face me.

The recording is paused, the camera pointing at a table of five individuals who are laughing and joking between themselves, oblivious to the fact they are being taped.

'This is a video from one of the CCTV cameras in the Ragamuffin Bar, taken on the day Simon died. Can you identify the people in the image for the purposes of the recording please?'

I lean forward, a fleeting twist of surprise tearing at my gut. 'That's Simon, with Bec, Hayley, David – and me. When was this taken?'

'At twelve thirty-five. Before you went across the road to the escape room, you all met here for drinks first. Do you remember?'

'No.'

'Are you sure?'

I splutter a nervous laugh. 'I think I'd remember that. The prices are astronomical.'

And then I realise I've seen a transaction on my

online bank statement for that day, but it wasn't listed under the name of a bar. It was something like Flatt and Adams. Was that the company who owned the bar Forbes is talking about?

Forbes presses on regardless and hits the play button.

'This is from a second camera that's in the corner to the left of the table you were all sitting around. Watch closely.'

I sit, my eyes fixed on the screen as the recording plays out, and then I raise my gaze to hers after two minutes. 'What?'

Forbes rewinds the recording and moves around the table so she's standing between me and my solicitor. Mortlock joins us, his curiosity piqued. Evidently, he hasn't seen this recording before, either.

Forbes provides the commentary as the recording starts again. 'You leave the table here – I presume you're going to the toilet.'

I disappear from the camera's view, and a few seconds later Forbes taps her forefinger against the screen. 'Here, when Simon leaves the table to go to the toilet as well. Watch David.'

We do, in silence.

He reaches into his pocket and pulls out a tiny

plastic bag – it's only just visible on the video, but it's there.

'Notice how neither Bec nor Hayley seem to question what he's doing,' says Forbes.

David opens the bag, removes something from it and holds his hand above Simon's drink. He glances over his shoulder. Then he looks at each of them in turn.

Bec nods.

Hayley nods.

David's fingers open, and then he picks up the glass and swirls the drink around a few times, placing the glass back on the table.

I gasp, the sound echoing off the interview room walls and sit back, my mouth open.

'Keep watching,' Forbes tells me.

Next, Hayley reaches into her handbag and pulls out a bottle of water. David repeats the action with that, then hands it back to her. Hayley screws the cap back on, shakes the bottle and then puts it in her bag as Simon returns to the table.

Forbes reaches out and hit the stop button. She leaves the laptop open, the image frozen on Simon sitting back on his bar stool, and reaches into the manila folder for another document.

She scans the contents while my heartbeat thuds

in my ears, and then she reads out the name of a substance from the report.

'Known as a date-rape drug,' she says, 'because it leaves the system after a few hours and can't be easily traced at post-mortem. Nor did anyone pick it up during the transplant process. However, if it's mixed with alcohol in large enough quantities, it can kill. It induces a heart attack. We went back to the escape room before the bins were emptied by the council last week and found the bottle that contained traces of the water Hayley and David spiked.'

The solicitor lowers his head and scribbles furiously across his notebook.

'I didn't kill Simon,' I say, my voice is shaking. 'I would never have condoned that. You said it yourself. Hayley and David were the ones who put the drug in his drinks.'

'Oh, I saved the best part for last,' says Forbes. She hits the play button once more.

At that moment, I appear on screen from the same direction Simon went in. I sit on a chair with my back to the camera.

There's no sound, but I watch as Simon points to the drink before him, makes some sort of comment – probably to the effect that he suspects his friends have done something to his drink for a prank – and we all shake our heads, laughing.

Then I reach out and pick up his cocktail. I take a huge swallow of the stuff, then slam it back on the table in front of him.

Simon takes the hint and downs the rest in three gulps, and much cheering takes place.

'It's why you can't remember what happened,' says Forbes. 'What with the painkillers you were on, that single gulp of drink contained enough of the date-rape drug to tip you over the edge. The rest of it killed Simon. You were the one who encouraged him to drink it.'

'I didn't know!' I turn in my seat to face my solicitor. 'You saw what happened – I wasn't there when they spiked his drink. I didn't know what they put in it. I must have thought it was something harmless, that it was just for a laugh.'

Forbes ignores my outburst. 'We've interviewed the owner of the escape room. The lights going out at that part in the game was part of the script. It was only bad luck on Simon's part that the effects of the date-rape drug kicked in then. Bad luck, because the cameras in the room didn't pick up enough detail on the night vision setting for the owner to raise the alarm until you all started panicking and banging on the door to be let out.' Forbes closes the laptop. 'What they did manage to find for us was footage of Hayley passing that bottle of water to Simon as you all played the first game, and Simon drinking from that bottle. Rather than rehydrate him, of course, it topped up the levels of the date rape drug in his system, killing him.'

I'm frozen in my seat, my hands clasped together, knuckles white.

'I think Bec had second thoughts after we interviewed her,' says Forbes. 'I think she was going to come back to us and tell us what really happened. I think the guilt was getting to her with what happened to Simon and – who knows? – maybe she was contemplating coming back and telling us about Greg as well. Except David got to her first. He went around to her house to find out what her intentions were, but when he got there and found her in the bath he decided it was an opportunity he couldn't miss. He tried to silence her permanently.'

'But she lived.'

'Like I said before, she's a very lucky woman. He didn't mean for her to survive. He didn't hold her under the water long enough, and despite his best efforts he didn't slice through any major arteries. It's why the paramedics were able to save her, and why it looked like a pitiful attempt to take her own life, rather than the attempted murder it really was, especially after he'd leaked the story about her arrest to Scott Nash. Everyone was to assume she'd taken her own life after the news story broke. We originally wanted to re-interview her in the hospital about what she remembers of that day.' Forbes shakes her head, a sense of wonder in her voice. 'Rebecca decided to tell us a lot more. I guess a second chance at life meant a lot more to her than it did to you.'

I recoil at the dig, but say nothing.

Mortlock's heard enough. He shuffles in his seat, and then I hear him inhale before he begins to speak.

'Lisa Ashton, you do not have to say anything …'

THREE MONTHS LATER

THE STEEL DOOR shudders into place, and a moment later the rattle of a bolt and a key turning in the lock reaches my ears.

I sink onto the thin mattress and stare at the wall opposite my bunk bed as the sounds of a prison being secured for the night echo around me.

It's the waiting that's been the worst.

Mortlock and Forbes arranged for police divers to search the lake again as soon as they'd corroborated my statement with those of Bec and Hayley.

I couldn't answer the question of why we didn't tell anyone at the time what had happened.

I've tried to reason with myself that we were in shock, terrified, but as the weeks have passed I've realised that the fear didn't stem from the police finding out – it was what David or Simon would do if we went to them in the first place.

When Greg disappeared into the cold dark water of the lake that night, I became a recluse. I shunned attention from other men for years because I ached for him, longed to talk to someone about what had happened.

Except I didn't, because David had forbade it, and then it was too late.

Too much time had passed.

Our biggest mistake in all of this was underestimating him. As our group contracted and we shut ourselves away from anyone else all those years ago at university, David became the keeper of secrets.

Simon was impossible to talk to – sullen, bitter, and regretful that he'd backed up David and never allowed us to admit to what had happened all those years ago. He always believed it was his fault for suggesting the swimming race in the first place.

So, David became our confidant when we

thought life was treating us unfairly. He was the quiet one, who didn't gossip and always offered a shoulder to cry on when things went wrong.

We trusted him.

Except he banked that information and waited. Waited until the right moment came to execute his plan.

During Hayley's trial, her solicitor informed the jury she had been blackmailed by Simon, who threatened to reveal her shoplifting habits. She claimed she had no choice. She had confided in David, who had bided his time, waiting to turn that fear into something he could use to his advantage.

Such as murder.

When he found out I was dying and that he would never have me for his own unless Simon donated a kidney, David sought out Hayley's help first.

Reasoning that her pent-up need for revenge would make her an easy target, he set in motion a plan that had been in the making for years.

Starting with the death of Greg Fisher.

I think once Forbes started to look into Simon's death and questioned all of us, Hayley began to wonder what had really happened in the lake that night.

Why David had urged her to swim away, to leave him with Greg.

The police divers spent a day and a night trawling the thick silt and debris that lined the lakebed, with more care than had been taken the last time. I chewed my nails to the quick as I waited in my cell for news and wondered what could have been if Greg hadn't died.

My mind played tricks – what if he wasn't dead? What if he had simply disappeared? What if it was an accident?

It was Forbes who came to the remand wing of the prison and sat opposite me and my solicitor to break the news.

A body had been recovered, too rotten and decomposed to be identifiable by anything other than dental records after being found snagged on an old iron post lodged in the bottom of the former gravel pit. His parents had been informed by Police Scotland, and a funeral service was to be held in Glasgow. They had never moved away, terrified that if they did, their missing son wouldn't know where to return.

I cried myself to sleep that night.

Dread replaced hope four weeks ago as my

solicitor began to report back from the other hearings.

David has already been sentenced; the jury took less than two hours to reach their verdict according to my mum.

Hayley didn't fare much better and is now serving her sentence at a women's prison in Peterborough, and, like me, Bec is being held on remand while she waits for a sentencing date.

At least I have the cell to myself, and for that I'm grateful. It gives me time to think.

As the preparation for my trial progressed, the memories gradually returned. Not all of them; I still don't remember everything that went on in the escape room, despite seeing the CCTV evidence from the Ragamuffin Bar.

My solicitor has drawn heavily on the fact that Simon's drink was spiked without my knowledge in order to try and win some sympathy from those who hold my future in their hands.

Whether they will forgive me for remaining silent about Greg's disappearance remains to be seen, especially after what has come to light about David's involvement in his death.

I think Hayley started to have second thoughts about the plan to kill Simon; that's why his dad saw her arguing with him outside the café the day before his death. Perhaps it was her last attempt to make him see sense, to offer him life instead of the death sentence she knew had been planned for him.

If only he'd agreed to be a living donor.

I don't think she had the strength to stand up to David, to tell him to stop, to tell him the idea she said she'd thought he'd first suggested as a joke had gone too far.

If Forbes hadn't turned up at Mum and Dad's house when she did, I'm sure I'd be dead, too and that David would have gone in search of Hayley next, because by then she'd told him I was desperate for information about the exact circumstances of Greg's death and in danger of exposing his darkest secret without even realising it.

What about Bec, then?

Simon had been gaslighting her for years, ever since they'd first started going out. Coercing her into handing over her life savings only to lose the lot had taken her to breaking point. When David suggested a permanent solution, she realised she had a way out.

She simply didn't expect the guilt to catch up with her quite so quickly afterwards, or realise that David could no longer be trusted as a confidant.

When David realised she was a liability, he attempted to kill her as well, to stop her going back to the police and telling Forbes about her suspicions regarding a missing persons case involving Greg Fisher.

The truth about why David attacked me hit me hard when my solicitor told me an hour ago, and I scratch at my skin to try to alleviate the crawling sensation across my flesh.

David has had me in his sights for years, according to his statement. Biding his time while he tried to summon enough courage to share his feelings.

Because David wanted me.

Because Simon knew that, laughed at him, and told him he didn't stand a chance. And then two years ago had an affair with me to prove it.

David never forgave him.

He'd already killed once to remove someone who he saw as a competitor for my attention, and it seems another death caused him no concern at all if it meant saving me. He simply had to coerce Hayley and Bec into believing it was for the best.

And, because of how Simon had treated them, they did.

Afterwards, he spent the days after Simon's

death sowing the seeds of doubt in my mind, creating a chasm between Hayley, Bec and me so in the end I was estranged from them and only had David to turn to.

It nearly worked, except I told him my life expectancy was still shortened, despite the transplant, which wouldn't last for ever.

Despite his killing Simon.

Despite his trying to save my life.

And it seemed that he was tired of waiting for me and too scared to lose me forever, so he attacked.

According to my solicitor, the judge told David he'd be lucky to be free by his sixtieth birthday, and I wonder how I will manage to cover my tracks after all this so he can't find me when he gets out.

Because he scares me.

I've realised, listening to my solicitor, that David has been obsessed with me for over seven years and I haven't even realised. Who else might he have harmed if they'd stood in his way? What would have happened if I'd fallen for someone else if my life hadn't been turned upside down by my illness?

And so, to me.

Because, even though I didn't see what David did to Simon's drink, I should have warned him. I had no idea what David had put in it and yet I was the one who encouraged Simon to finish it.

And I was the one who benefited from his death.

The jury is out now, contemplating my future. In the meantime, I have to sit here and wait to be sentenced. There are procedures to follow, paperwork to file, promises to make.

My solicitor tells me I'll get a light sentence. Maybe four years for good behaviour.

That's okay.

I can live with that.

THE END

AFTERWORD

Dear Reader

I hope you've enjoyed reading *The Friend Who Lied*.

I've had a fascination with locked room mysteries for a number of years, and in between reading some favourite thrillers and crime fiction, I've devoured a lot of psychological suspense.

Writing *The Friend Who Lied* enabled me to combine those two loves into one story, and I had a lot of fun writing it.

Thanks to Keshini Naidoo for reading an early draft and providing valuable feedback, and to Donna Hillyer for her work in bringing the manuscript to life as well as providing advice about organ donation and the transplant process. Julia

Gibbs is, as always, a formidable proofreader and an integral part of my team.

Thanks to my writing friends who provided encouragement along the way – a special thank you to Rachel Abbott, Shalini Boland, Robert Bryndza, Adam Croft, Lisa Hall, Caroline Mitchell and Mel Sherratt for being at the end of an email and giving me a thumbs up or a kick when I needed it.

Finally, but of course by no means least, thank you to my amazing readers and the book blogging community. I couldn't do any of this without you, and it's because of you I turn up for work in the writing cave every morning.

Thanks again for reading *The Friend Who Lied*. If you enjoyed it, please consider leaving a review – it really is the best way to help me spread the word about my writing.

Thank you.

Rachel Amphlett

www.rachelamphlett.com

CPSIA information can be obtained
at www.ICGtesting.com
Printed in the USA
BVHW071522030619
549982BV00005B/796/P

9 781999 368340